THRONE OF THE BASTARDS

BRIAN KEENE
STEVEN L. SHREWSBURY

TPB ISBN 978-1-937009-60-1

Cover art © Daniel Kamarudin.

Jacket design by Justin Stewart.

Published by Apex Publications, LLC, PO Box 24323, Lexington, KY 40524

Visit us at www.apexbookcompany.com.

With admiration and respect to ...

Robert E. Howard, Karl Edward Wagner
Manly Wade Wellman, Clark Ashton Smith
H.P. Lovecraft, Edgar Rice Burroughs

And

Our sons

For the spirit of the storm flows in their veins, too ...

THE SAGA OF ROGAN, OR, WHAT HAS GONE BEFORE

Rogan, born in a savage age before the great flood, was sliced from his mother's belly by his father, Jarek. Raised into barbarism among the fabled Keltos folk in the Caucaus Mountains, Rogan accepted violence as a simple way of life.

Roaming the lands north of the Black Sea, Rogan grew strong amongst his rugged kin. He soon wearied of a life disrupting the obsidian trade from the east, and raiding the great cities of Chanoch, Urak and Jericho. So Rogan journeyed west, crossing the land bridge at Bosporus. The accounts of his adventures during this time have been thought lost in the deluge, but recently pieced together by Miskatonic professor Elijah Blackthorn.

Eventually, Rogan became a mercenary for King Akhensobek, ruler of Kemet. Rogan lead the king's armies, until a tryst with the royal daughter aroused Akhensobek's ire. As punishment, Rogan was walled up alive inside the great idol of the reclining cat god, Bastet. After a miraculous escape, Rogan slew the king, his 150 children and returned to the primal kingdoms of the north.

Cutting a bloody swath through the lesser realms of Lascaux,

Agudea, and Gordes, Rogan became a leader in the revolutionary forces of General Thyssen in Albion. The two men became great friends and comrades at arms. Thyssen wished to oust Silex, the cruel ruler of the realm of Albion. The revolution ended when Rogan seized the crown from Silex's decapitated head and placed it on his own.

Rogan's rule of Albion ran stern but fair. Thyssen was given command of Albion's military might. Border clashes with native Prytens and their savage Queen Tancorix kept them busy for decades. Rogan wed Thyssen's sister, Desna, and sired an heir, Rohain. Several more children followed and Rogan came to know contentment, however fleetingly. After the death of Queen Desna in childbirth, however, Rogan grew weary of palace life and abdicated his throne to Rohain.

Accompanied by his nephew Javan, the youngest son of General Thyssen, and his bodyguards, Rogan journeyed across the western ocean, discovering fabled lands and great cultures far to the south in the new world, beyond the edges of scholar's maps. There, Rogan set about adventuring again with the aid of fresh friends from the mysterious realm of Olmek-Tikal.

Attacked on the sea by raiders from his former kingdom, Rogan fights with Karza—a warrior who claims to be his son. Karza tells Rogan that his brother, supposedly another of Rogan's bastard sons, has toppled Rohain from the throne of Albion. Rogan kills Karza, with some assistance from Javan. In the great ensuing fight, wrought with monsters and the magic of Damballah, only Rogan and Javan survive, shipwrecked. They are soon befriended by the Kennebeck folk, natives of the land, and their shaman, Akibeel. Javan becomes romantically involved with a young warrior named Zenata.

In an effort to return to his kingdom, Rogan agrees to help Akibeel, whose folk are threatened by a dire time traveling wizard on a mountain, who brings forth a member of the Thirteen, Meeble, to that reality. While Javan and the Kennebeck battle the monsters and minions of the wizard, Rogan engages Meeble in hand to hand combat, successfully pushing him through a portal and back into the Labyrinth.

When Captain Xuxan, an old friend from Olmek-Tikal, finds them, Rogan—now joined by Akibeel and his Kennebeck warriors—vows to go back to his overturned kingdom and spill light and blood on the shadows that grip it ...

"*And those of the demonic horde laughed at the words of the Wiseman in the seventh heaven. And yet, he spoke to us with great scorn.*

Woe to those who build up kingdoms of iniquity and oppression; and who lay their foundations in fraud. For suddenly, they will be subverted, never to obtain peace.

Woe to you who build up houses on crime; for they will have foundations that break and by their swords they themselves shall fall.

You have committed great blasphemy and iniquity and are destined to the day of effusion of blood, unto the day of darkness, and to the day of great judgment.

This I declare and point out to you, that he who created you will destroy you."

From Fragment XXVI of the Fourth Yee-Wa

PROLOGUE

ANOTHER PRELUDE TO A YARN

The great vessel heaved, sending the man and his attentive children sprawling to the deck. A spray of salt water washed over the edge, dousing them all. At first, the children laughed. Then, when they saw the black-red serrated pincers appear out of the foam and snap the vessel's rail, they screamed.

"You know the drill," the man shouted as he dropped to his knees. "Tubal, grab the swords! Gomer, you look alive! Tiras and Magog, to his side!"

Tubal, a dark-haired youth of ten summers went into a roll across the deck, not even trying to rise, and stopped his progress by bouncing against a large butcher's block sporting many leather-bound pommels. He righted himself and started to yank the handles out, throwing them at his brothers and father.

The ship groaned, careening sharply to one side as the clawed thing tried to heave its bulk aboard. Water streamed from its carapace. It waved one clawed arm in the air, snapping its massive pincers together and making a terrible sound.

CLICK-CLICK ... CLICK-CLICK ...

Tubal paused, gaping. His eyes went from the monster to his brothers, and then back to the monster again. He spotted a stinger-equipped tail jutting from the water.

"Back to the deep," their father shouted as he slashed at one of the creature's spindly legs, cracking the chitinous coating and cleaving into the flesh beneath. The beast screeched and slipped backwards. The big man sawed his sword back and forth, cleaving through the appendage.

CLICK-CLICK ... CLICK-CLICK ...

Though maimed, the monstrosity pulled itself up further, using its claws to grip the great boat. The boys attacked these, slamming their small blades—cast for children—against the hard shell. The creature's eyes, like two black balls suspended on stalks, goggled at them. It opened its beak-like mouth and hissed.

One of the boys stabbed down into the claw as if he were digging a post hole for a fence. Grinning, he twisted his weapon and yelled, "Wodan!"

"Here now, Gomer!" Their father backhanded the youth, aiming for the top of his head but slapping him flat in the face, sending him careening ass over elbows to the deck. "Speak not the name of the old gods."

Tubal, a head taller than the others, stepped up and executed a clean slash across the monster's face, severing both eyestalks, while his father hacked at the claws.

"He pretends to be Grandfather," Tubal explained. "He's playing around."

Their father rolled his eyes. "I better tell you to tales of your pious grandsire, from now on, rather than stories about the King of Albion. Tiras, look alive!"

Their father cleaved through one claw. Gomer rose, nose bleeding, but a smile on his face. Blood dripped onto his teeth as his lips parted.

"For Grandfather Rogan!" He stabbed again at the other claw. The monster let go of the deck and seized the boy's sword instead. As it toppled back into the ocean, Gomer almost went with him.

When he released his sword hilt, he fell sprawling to the deck again.

The beast sank beneath the churning sea, turning the froth red with its blood, and taking the youth's sword with it.

"Boy, I swear by the God of Heaven ..." Their father gripped Gomer by the right arm and heaved him upright. "You've lost another weapon."

"I'm sorry, father."

"I should make another son and leave the rest of you to the spawn of the Dark Ones."

Tubal gaped over the edge of the ship and then drew back. "Are those really what those beasts are, father?"

"Aye. Cattle for the Dark Ones. Livestock. Beasts of both burden and war. I imagine this one wandered astray. You seldom see them above the waves. Rogan fought one, long ago."

"Tell us more." Gomer spat blood on the deck.

"No," argued Tubal. "We have another story of our grandfather to finish first. Tell us more of what happened when he returned to Albion."

"Yes!" Tiras gushed as Magog settled in beside him. "You told us the beginning of the tale. Now tell us the rest!"

Their father yawned and shrugged. "You all deserve a further tale?"

Tubal fetched a towel and started to clean off the blades. "We have some time, father."

Gomer leaned forward. "How did Albion fall so easily under the usurper from the dark continent, Karac?"

"Yes," Tubal nodded. "You were vague on that, father."

"There are more details, dire and dark, ones that came unto your grandfather in dreams as he returned across the sea."

The boys all said as one, "Tell us, father."

"Get me something to drink, and not water. I want one of those vessels your living grandfather hides by the sheep ... and thinks himself stealthy."

Tubal grinned and ran to the lower decks.

The other children gathered in as their father leaned back and took a breath.

Once the wine arrived, he said, "Ready?"

Smiles all about, the children, now supplemented by a few of their sisters, settled in as the ship rocked.

"King Rogan and the natives from Olmek-Tikal traveled back to Albion on the great ship brought by Xuxan from the south. In his dreams, your grandfather Rogan became haunted by the events in Albion, events he never could've seen, save for the wizardry of the native's shaman, Akibeel. But the reality of what awaited them upon their arrival was far worse than any nightmare ..."

CHAPTER 1
THE WELCOMING COMMITTEE

"Is there no one among you who will stand against this beast? I suppose I'll have to kill it myself."

The creature shrieked, lurching forward on the deck of the heaving ship. While it may have walked like a man, and was humanoid in shape—possessing two arms and two legs—it was anything but human, sporting the head of a squid and a writhing beard of tentacles. More tentacles thrashed around its groin, and its skin was a sickly pale-green hue. It took another squelching step, but a sword swung in the strained light, drawing blood. The monster screamed in response to being cut. The thick limbed man holding the sword cursed. The beast's flipper feet skated on the deck, but it didn't back down, despite its injury.

"Be cautious, Rogan," shouted Xuxan.

Ignoring the advice, the gray-bearded man swung his sword again. Cries arose from the crew as he missed. Their dismay turned to screams as the back of the creature rippled and moved. Dozens of tiny spawn jumped off the monster and onto the rolling deck, skittering in all directions like spiders.

"Fuck," Rogan shouted as he slashed down, sword sideways, using the flat of the blade to squash one of the tiny creatures.

"Fuck! Fuck! Fuck!" With every expletive, he crushed another rambling baby.

Enraged, their parent roared, swiping at him with clawed hands. Its tentacles whipped through the air, grasping for the swordsman.

"Damn you bastards," Rogan yelled at the gaping sailors. "Don't stand there with your dicks in your hands! *Strike!*"

The men, all truly stunned at the horror from the sea, held up their bows and drew back. In a moment, a dozen arrows perforated the squid-thing. It squalled and staggered while the big man continued to crush the babies springing from its back. He stomped around the deck, his boots drenched in gore. A young man stepped near him. This youth took careful aim and pulled back his bow, releasing his arrow and striking the squid-monster through the right eye. The beast stumbled backward against the rail, flailing. The young man quickly swung his bow on his back and faced Rogan. From his belt the youth took a dangling axe. Twin heads were attached to the pommel. He offered this weapon to the older warrior.

"What do I want with that, Javan?" Rogan shook his head as the other sailors joined in stomping.

Javan shrugged and pushed the axe on him. "You are stronger than I, sire. You can wield it easier."

Snatching the axe handle from Javan's hand and handing him the sword, Rogan snorted, "I'm not your king. How many times must I tell you that, nephew?"

Javan struggled with the heavy sword, but didn't let it fall to the deck. A tall lad, but built nothing like the tree-trunk his uncle resembled, the broadsword wasn't something Javan could use with great skill.

"Then strike, Rogan," Javan said simply, like a butler offering tea and biscuits. "Cut that thing in half. It's still moving, and we haven't had breakfast yet."

Rogan planted his boots on the wet deck, trying to find his footing amidst sea water and blood. He took the axe handle in both hands and drew the weapon up over his head. Rogan grinned as he prepared for the strongest throw of his life. Screeching, the creature turned itself about and prepared to leap back into the sea from which it had originated.

"No, you don't," Rogan yelled, axe still held aloft, and ran after the beast, swinging the twin-headed axe before the thing could clamber over the side. The weapon fell awkwardly, cleaving in-between the tentacles that hung down the creature's back like locks of hair ... but the axe found a home, straight down where a man's spinal column should be. It cleaved the flesh like butter, ripping loose and opening the skin down to the thing's buttocks. Staggering, the monster fell to the gore-spattered deck, reaching feebly for the rail with one trembling hand, while more of the tiny spawn leaped from their dying host. They tumbled into the churning ocean, vanishing beneath the froth.

"I hit him where Wodan split him!" Roaring with laughter, Rogan stepped on the left leg of the jittering beast and then planted his other boot on the ruined right buttock. The move caused the huge wound he'd just created to gape more. A foul odor escaped, making all of the sailors draw back. Rogan's jovial expression soured.

Javan gagged, fanning his nose. "By the goddess ..."

"Aye," Rogan agreed. "Smells like the outhouse by the last whorehouse in Irem."

"It is still moving, Uncle."

Rogan reared back and swung the axe, cutting right through the head of the beast. He applied pressure, grunting with the effort, until the skull split apart. The monster ceased thrashing, and lay still. Some of the sailors began heaving, while others finished off the miniscule spawn. Sighing, Rogan stepped away from the carcass. He handed the axe to Javan and took back his sword.

"What pussies," Rogan muttered, nodding at a retching sailor. "You would think sea dogs like these would have more guts, or at least one ball, when facing the sons of Cthulhu."

Javan, ever erudite, offered politely, "Perhaps they are young."

Rogan turned to eye the seaman, all sporting greasy black hair made stiff with the salt air. "They are far from home, Javan. The Kennebeck folk and the men from Olmek-Tikal, both. If they left their courage across the ocean, they better find their sacks before we land in Albion. They will need all the bravery they can muster."

Javan nodded.

"The sun is awake to greet us," Rogan barked. "It will be hot again today. Finish your breakfasts. You'll need the stamina."

As the sun rose, the scene froze in place like a painting ... and then faded.

ROGAN, JAVAN, AND THEIR CREW—WHICH CONSISTED OF BOTH seasoned sailors from Olmek-Tikal and the novice Kennebeck natives—sailed across the ocean with a powerful wind at their backs. Many times during their long journey they'd lashed themselves down to avoid being washed overboard. The tanned seafarers of Olmek-Tikal murmured that they had never experienced anything like it before. The red-skinned Kennebeck folk whispered among themselves that the wind was an extension of Rogan's anger—his will made manifest into the world. Their shaman, Akibeel, theorized that far off Albion and the old world that Rogan knew were also assailed by storms, and thus, they were caught up in the rush of the wind. Whatever the reason for the winds, they saw no rain, but appeared to have a great push from the gods, shoving the galley faster and faster, almost beyond the ability of the sailors to service it.

Javan reminded all of them that a regular trip from Albion across the ocean to the islands of southern Olmek-Tikal usually took nearly two months. However, since they were far north of the islands, Javan calculated their trip to be a much shorter one.

"I never counted on the breath of the gods at our back," Javan said as he looked into the brunt of the rushing wind. "We are making excellent time. We should reach Albion quicker than we had expected."

Rogan took a swig of wine—keenly aware that it was the last skin of such on the vessel, but keeping that information to himself —and said, "Here is where I would say a bawdy joke about the gods blowing me, but I am not in the mood for it. Also, I suspect you have bad news to go with the good."

Javan nodded, shoulders slumping.

For three weeks they had battled the ocean, the winds, and the occasional monster. The Kennebeck men had proven poor sailors at first, spending much of their time heaving over the edge of the craft or cowering and screaming in fear of whatever creature the sea vomited up, but in time they adjusted. The more experienced crewman from Olmek-Tikal helped them adjust.

"Well? Out with it, lad." Rogan drained the rest of the wine, tossed the empty skin over the side, and belched. "Give me the bad news. Are we still on course?"

The son of Thyssen looked at the fading moon and shielded his eyes against the rising sun. In the far distance, swirling clouds were visible, but the sky over their heads was clear.

"We are off course, sire," Javan confessed. "At this rate, we shall not make the southern ports of Condaten."

"Curse the gods!" Rogan raged, his gray beard bristling as he thrashed around. The sailors suppressed laughter at this act. Rogan sneered at them. "Don't get your humor from me, you little pricks. Worry more about holding your guts firm in these waters. Or better yet, go boil your balls."

Xuxan, a leader in far-off Olmek-Tikal who now served as captain of the ship, snorted as he waved at the sky. "The gods favor you, Rogan. Holding your tongue may not be a bad idea."

"If I were a younger man, I'd knock your skinny ass down and brawl for that, Xuxan. But wrestling this ship is enough fight for one day. How far off are we, Javan?"

Javan hesitated. "You intended to return via the ports south of Albion in Gaulla-Argonus by Condaten, correct?"

Rogan nodded. "At least there we would have safe harbor and a direct line back to my ... the kingdom. We would find if these tales from those bastards are all true or not. Where are we heading instead?"

Javan frowned. "As I said, at such a rapid pace, we are making incredible time, but—"

"I don't care about that. Where are we heading?"

"We are being sent farther north into the Prytenish wilderness."

"Wodan," Rogan spat, not expecting an answer from his grim god.

"Sire," Javan said gently. "Your exploits with the Pryten savage, Queen Tancorix, were legendary decades ago. Surely, that bit of goodwill guarantees us safe travel through their wasteland?"

Blue eyes fixed east as if he could see the Prytenish lands, Rogan remained deep in thought for some time. The sailors, sensing that his mood had passed, returned to their duties. Only Javan and Xuxan remained by his side, waiting in silence. Akibeel sat cross-legged nearby, gumming a piece of jerky.

"Tancorix ..." Rogan's voice was lower than before, almost grave. "You speak her name as if she wasn't a force of nature, Javan. While the vile Pryten savages listen to the will of their queen, she is not a policeman dire to inflict her will on them every day. The wilderness is vast, thus, a new breed of Pryten may never have heard of our exploits."

"But they told stories about you to their children."

"One can only get so far on legend, Javan. After that ... sometimes, you must write a new interval in blood." He glanced back at the crew and frowned. "I don't know if this force can live through such a journey. The Kennebeck are fierce warriors and these men of Olmek-Tikal have proven hardy, but our numbers are but a drop in this damned ocean compared to our foes."

"Surely, Tancorix—"

Rogan cut him off. "What is Rohain's relationship with those in Prytendom? I cannot afford to base my plans on the life expectancy of a barbarian queen. Who knows if she has been slain or deposed by now?"

Javan sighed. "I told you of Rohain's brief border war with the Prytens that started over their wizard class kidnapping your son Teran in a bid to keep Albion from expanding?"

"Aye." Rogan nodded. "Rohain beat them into submission as far as he dare go into their wilderness. What did Tancorix say of that border fight?"

"Teran proved resourceful in his escape, sire, and also discovered that not all Prytens worship the Druid class or listen to the edicts of Tancorix. Though a youth, Teran fought his way to the marshes and formed a few alliances in the Pryten tribes loyal to Tancorix."

"Yes," Rogan snapped, impatient. "If you want to tell long stories, tell them to that warrior girl, Zenata, whom you hole up with below decks. What are you getting at?"

Javan frowned. "That if we must land, perhaps these Prytens of the marshes in the wilderness near Albion will be more hospitable to the father of Teran than to the father of Rohain."

"Bah, we cannot trust the Prytens, no matter who I screwed to make peace twenty years ago!" Rogan gritted his teeth. "They are worse savages than ... well, than the men of the mountains where I was born. If my destiny is to be decided by the Prytens, then we have already lost."

Rising from his perch, Akibeel walked slowly across the deck of the ship, teetering as he went. A red brave helped him move. Rogan, Javan, and Xuxan watched him approach. Sea birds circled overhead, squawking. A school of small, silver fish jumped from the spray, shimmering in the dawn.

"Rogan," Akibeel said, "I have seen visions of your land, and your nephew speaks the truth. For you to judge the barbarians of Prytendom so harshly is wrong."

"Damnations be unto you wizards," Rogan growled. "You cannot be happy with this world so much so that you pierce through to the next. Be gone from my sight, old man! Your visions may show you things, but they don't teach you history. It was a larger bag of gold that made me rend Albion from its King years ago, instead of leading the Pryten uprising. Perhaps I erred then and would not be in this place now if I stayed with my own kind ... barbarians ..."

Akibeel persisted. "Rogan, barbarians aplenty will aide your son in his venture to reclaim his crown, though not only from Prytendom."

"What say you?"

"I have seen a gnarled old leader—older than even myself— plotting in the mountains north of your kingdom. Also, a great force of red-haired warriors are spilling into the northern wilderness of the Prytens."

The ship's bow dropped suddenly, tossed on a wave. Ocean spray coursed over the vessel, wetting them all. Despite this, Rogan's mouth grew dry.

"North?" He leaned forward, staring at the shaman intently. "Those of Cramonds? They guard our north border. Red-haired? Those from Thule farther on up?"

Akibeel shrugged. "I know not the names of your land. These ... Cramonds?"

"Yes," Javan confirmed. "That is their name."

"These Cramonds plot with your elite warriors," Akibeel said. "The ones who fled your kingdom. They are joined by a group of hairy barbarians."

Rogan faced Javan. "A gnarled old leader? Looks like your father made it out of Karac's venture, eh?"

Javan tried to fight off a prideful smile. "Thyssen would."

Rogan pondered this. "So, when oppressed, Rohain's loyalists returned to the land of his kindred. Interesting. Perhaps I was wrong to curse the gods, after all. Perhaps Wodan will draw all under his blessing together. Heh. Under my ass, he will! What else do you see, Akibeel? What of the rest of my family? Erin and Algeniz and Teran?"

Sighing, Akibeel sat down next to him on the wet planks. He

moaned, making a big show of effort.

"Enough of that," Rogan muttered. "Your bones ache no worse than mine."

"This salt air is no good for my joints," Akibeel sighed. "And it does nothing to help your disposition, either."

Rogan glared at him. "I liked it better when you couldn't speak my language and Javan had to translate for you."

Suppressing a laugh, Akibeel closed his eyes and breathed deeply. The three men watched him as he went into a trance. After a moment, he began to speak, his voice low. They had to strain to hear him over the roar of the ocean and the creaking ship.

"Your daughters are in your kingdom, unharmed but worried, and I see your other boy, Teran, returning to them."

"Shit fire and save the flints." Rogan frowned. "What is he doing alone?"

Akibeel shook his mane of greasy hair from side to side. "I cannot see."

"Why not, blast it?"

"Because, your bright kingdom grows darker. He is ... hunted? Hunting?"

Rising to his feet, Rogan walked to the edge of the heaving vessel and gripped the side-rails near the catapult. "Javan, how long until we arrive?"

"You keep asking, uncle."

"You are not telling, nephew."

"Normally, this trip would take many weeks, even with these sailors venturing into such uncharted waters for them."

"But? Spit it out."

"In a handful of days, we will be in the range of the Prytens."

Rogan understood him. The closer they drew to the coast the more likely they would be as targets of Pryten reavers.

"Let them come then. Let every pirate and raider find us here. This salt water is making my hair hard and my tongue thirsty."

But it wasn't water he craved, for the only thing to remedy the thirsts of the warrior King was blood.

SEVERAL MORE DAYS PASSED, AND THE WINDS NEVER CEASED. The vessel plowed ahead, day and night, bouncing over the waves, drawing ever nearer to the Prytenish coast. During that time, the crew discovered that someone had drank the last skin of wine, and there was much rumbling among them.

One morning, while Javan and Zenata were watching the sunrise, they spotted a flock of large birds flying overhead, indicating that land was near. Within an hour, many distant craft appeared on the horizon—almost indistinguishable at first to all but the keen-eyed youth, but quickly taking shape as they sped toward them.

Captain Xuxan's body language showed no fear or apprehension. He casually strolled over to Rogan. "These are the reavers you spoke of?"

Grunting, the hulking old barbarian king stared at him with scorn.

"Aye, Xuxan," Javan piped up. "They take us for more of a merchant ship, not counting on us ready to deal war."

"Then they will be mistaken," Xuxan affirmed. "I will not be pirated by the likes of these rabble from the forests. Stinking tree-people ..."

"Sire?" Javan turned to Rogan. "I wonder if it would stop this impending attack if they knew of you and Tancorix?"

Rogan snorted. "Shall I pull out my manhood and wave it at them? See if they recognize my cock?"

Javan shrugged. "It couldn't hurt, I suppose."

"I imagine there are many who would recognize it," Zenata quipped.

Ignoring them, Rogan turned to the captain. "Prepare to unleash the catapults, Xuxan. There are too many to kill in my homeland. I won't be boarded or delayed by these scum!"

Nodding, Xuxan turned away and began barking orders at his men. Akibeel parroted him, translating for the members of the

Kennebeck tribe. As the sailors scrambled to their tasks, Rogan leaned close to Javan, his whiskers only inches from the boy's ear.

"We must get our bearings, lad."

"I'm working on it, sire. It is difficult with no land on which to gauge our location."

"My ... I mean Rohain's ... kingdom is in peril, and I'll be damned if a few Prytens interfere with our passage."

"Argonus would've been preferable, sire."

"Yes, blast it, and so would Albion, but the sea doesn't go that goddamned far does it?" Rogan glanced at the small vessels approaching them, and then back to Javan. "I wonder if any alliances I have across the world will help Rohain?"

"Perhaps we should focus instead on the more immediate danger," Javan suggested.

"Bah."

Akibeel tottered over to them, choosing his steps carefully as the ship rocked and swayed. He placed a gnarled hand on Rogan's shoulder. The grizzled savage stared up at him, but allowed the gesture to remain.

"Your nephew speaks the truth," Akibeel advised. "Rogan, there is a great army of dark-skinned men marching for Albion. A massive column advancing from so far away. They intend to make your land their home. But that means nothing if we are to die here, so close to shore."

"I do not fear these pirates." Rogan rubbed his gray beard. "What I fear are your visions. Gods. When I sat on the throne, some of my advisors always worried over such an army from the southern jungles, but I dismissed it as nonsense. They could never arise as one and march that far. But now you say otherwise."

Akibeel nodded.

"Where are they?" Rogan asked.

"I know not your land names, but they have become more dispersed in numbers as they crossed a large savannah. They are like spirits and I cannot see them in full."

Xuxan shouted more orders, kicking a few of the sailors who

apparently didn't move fast enough for his liking. Akibeel translated for his people, and then turned back to Rogan and Javan. A great horn echoed across the waves as the reavers drew closer.

Frowning, Rogan stared at the deck, ignoring the onrushing ships. "Axum, Nubia, Shawbati, Ashanti, Dahomians, and Zimbabwe truly have the numbers, but never the brains to mount such an army. They are more pathetic primitives than ..." Rogan stopped. "Wodan curse me for underestimating the desire of those fucking savages."

"There is royalty and wisdom among them, sire—same as in Albion," Javan gently corrected his uncle, his eyes not leaving the advancing pirates. "And you must consider, there are many lands they need to march through. Surely, they will not just stroll into fair Albion past all of your borderland allies?"

"Not every leader will let them pass easy, of course," Rogan agreed. "Some will desire tribute. And I cannot see those southern bastards being of a disciplined military force not to want to plunder along the way. That will work to our advantage and it is probably why the country isn't overrun already. Not every alliance was forged in good faith or a hard cock. Some were born out of fear. But I doubt they will want a kingdom of these worshipers of the dark forces set up in fair Albion. If they pay no respect to my son, then I have no use for them."

As the reavers drew closer, Xuxan snorted, "Allies like that aren't much good, Rogan. Any kingdom that would drop that easily may not be worth saving."

Rogan gripped the handle of his sword and planted his feet on the deck. "Once this matter is dissolved, Rohain should remember his foes and make sure they pay the price. Fear is all they understand. Fear and blood. Now come, let us meet our welcoming committee."

And then, the reavers were upon them. Xuxan called out for battle stations. The Prytens, howling a war cry to instill fear, propelled their many short sailing craft alongside the ship. Rogan threw back his head and laughed at them. They were a sunburnt lot, long, filthy manes of hair, primal and pure.

Xuxan hurried to the rear of the vessel and eyed up his sights. He shouted an order. Flints were struck and fire spat on the ship near the rear of the catapults. Xuxan yelled another command and the first catapult released its load. The vessel lurched hard. A muck of tar and debris set aflame rocketed across the green sea and smashed into the first Pryten craft, setting several pirates aflame. The small sail crumbled and the fiery load passed through the rear of the tiny boat with ease. The black haired Prytens barely had time to shout as the nose of their boat jerked out of the water and started to descend.

"What a shot!" Javan exclaimed as the next catapult fired.

Zenata, the warrior maiden, joined him in his glee, looking up at the young man with dancing eyes.

"I wish my sister were here for this fight," she said.

"You miss Asenka." Javan replied.

"I always miss her. Especially during a battle. She loved a good fight."

Javan jabbed at the sky with his long bow. "I wish they were in range."

"A moment more and they will be," she said.

"But still not in range of my sword," Rogan muttered.

Another catapult fired. A flaming load sliced off a reaver's sail, but missed the ship. The half dozen Prytens onboard wore stunned expressions as they sailed in fast ... but not as stunned as the ones they wore when the Kennebeck warriors raised their bows and released. In an instant, these dozen Prytens were pierced with arrows that easily penetrated their light mail armor shirts.

A third reaver swung away from the vessel as a fourth was split in half by the next catapult load. When the other attackers veered away, calling off the attack and speeding toward the horizon, a cheer rippled through the travelers from afar.

"Save your strength," Rogan murmured. "There will be war a plenty for us all soon enough."

CHAPTER 2
HOMECOMING

After two more days' journey farther down the coast, Javan was confident that he had his bearings. They suffered a few more attacks from the Pryten pirates, but none of the raiding attempts were successful. They swiftly crushed each assault. Still, Xuxan fretted that they were running low on ammunition for the catapults. Rogan bemoaned the fact that they had run out of wine.

The ship made dock in a place called Monas—a crude, rustic, unincorporated port constructed basically to make landings easier for pirates. It occupied a narrow sliver of beach and was bordered by an oppressive, looming forest. A few huts and rough lean-tos dotted the dirty sand. Smoke rose from fading cook fires and chickens roamed freely, pecking at the ground, but otherwise, the place appeared to be empty. Xuxan hailed the camp as they pulled alongside the dock, but received no answer.

"I don't like it," Akibeel advised. "It may be a trap."

"Well, then." Rogan shrugged. "We should make haste to disembark. It would be impolite of us to keep them waiting."

Javan's eyes widened. "Really, uncle?"

"Aren't you always urging me to be more civilized? Is that not the act of a civilized man—to meet potential enemies with palaver and treaties rather than a fight?"

"I think we should try for another port," Zenata said.

"The next one is a full day's travel," Javan replied, "and in more hostile terrain than here."

"We need supplies," Xuxan said. "Wine, fresh meat rather than that salted stuff. Fruits. Is there a guarantee we'll get it here?"

"No," Javan admitted. "But there's not a guarantee we won't, either."

After a quick consultation and debate, Rogan, Javan, and Xuxan, dressed in armor and ready for a fight, went down the makeshift dock, expecting to be greeted by a pack of enraged Prytens.

"Be ready," Rogan muttered, his scarred knuckles curled around the hilt of his sword.

As they reached the center of the deserted camp, many men emerged from the forest. Each of them wore the armor and colors of the Albion military. Rogan, Javan, and the captain stopped in their tracks, surprised. Rogan and Javan relaxed when they saw the familiar colors and insignia, but Xuxan remained tense.

"It's okay, Captain," Javan assured him. "These are friends, though I am surprised to see them here."

The group drew closer. Rogan gasped when he spotted a young, brawny man of maybe twenty years walking toward him.

"Do you know him?" Xuxan asked.

"It can't be," Rogan murmured. "Thyssen? He'd be far older than this youth ..."

Javan touched Rogan's arm and shook his head. "No, uncle."

The young man stopped in front of them and smiled. He had long, dark hair and a bushy beard.

"Thyssen?" Rogan asked again, almost whispering.

"Nay, sire," answered the youth. "Not the one you recall. The last time you saw me, I was but a lad when you took my half-brother Javan on a trip with you!"

"By the gods ..." Rogan burst forward and gripped the young

man by the biceps. "Boone! Boone, the son of General Thyssen! You were but a pup last time I saw you."

Boone nodded, laughing. "Aye."

"I remember when you were born," Rogan said. "After a legion of girls, Wodan gave your father another boy with his handmaiden! By the ass of the great goddess, it is good to see you!"

Boone gave a respectful bow to his famous forbearer's memory. He adjusted his rugged tunic, but it was clear that this young man was a veteran of warfare. Though most of his body was abundant with hair, his shoulders and chest appeared bare. Rogan knew this came from the embrace of chain mail and how its coarse kiss would wear such a covering off if used enough.

Javan smiled. "Greetings, brother. It is good to see you again."

Boone eyed his half-brother and then smacked him on the shoulder. "Greetings yourself, young one! I see the sea and sun have burnt you well. Has Rogan made a man of you yet?"

"Time will tell, brother."

Rogan cocked his thumb at the ship. "I'd say Zenata back yonder has made a man out of him and then some."

Javan blushed.

"Zenata? Did you bring home a foreign bride, Javan?"

"N-no," Javan stammered.

"He's just rutting with her," Rogan answered. Then he laughed, and squeezed Boone's shoulder. "We are well met, Boone. I had not expected this."

"Where are the brothers, Wagnar and Harkon?" Boone craned his head, staring at the ship. "Are they still on board?"

"Nay," Rogan said. "Killed in the world across the ocean by Pryten pirates and the brother of Karac—a swine named Karza."

Boone's expression darkened. "Father aided you in all of your trials and wars. It is a shame that terror currently grips this land he helped to create."

Rogan withdrew his hand from the younger man's shoulder. "Then the tales of the shaman Akibeel are true? There is a usurper on the throne of Albion?"

"I do not know this Akibeel," Boone said.

Javan quickly summarized their journey to the far off lands, their alignment with the Kennebeck folk, and how they'd journeyed back home. Both Rogan and Xuxan waited impatiently during the telling. When Javan was finished, Boone nodded.

"The visions this shaman spoke of—they are true, to the best of my knowledge. I was far away when the revolution came. So much of the regular army fled into the wilderness as the leaders were assassinated or executed. The tales of the great dark bastard from the south are true, from what I hear, but I have never laid eyes on him."

"Damn," Rogan swore. "Karac ..."

"That is his name," Boone confirmed.

"It tastes like blood and shit in my mouth."

Xuxan stepped forward and lightly touched Rogan's arm. "Your orders?"

"Unload the men," Rogan replied. "Let them get land under their feet again. Boone, is there trade to be had here? They need supplies. And whores."

"Aye." Boone nodded. "This camp is just to throw off enemies. The real village of Monas lies deep in the forest. It is a hike, but worth it. There is food, fresh water, items to trade. Women— although they are Pryten women, and I'm certain you wouldn't want to lose any of your men's lives to their mating rituals."

"No," Rogan agreed. "There are few among them who could survive the ordeal. Perhaps Javan, or Captain Xuxan. Maybe old Akibeel."

"Well, as I said, there is food and drink."

"Wine?" Rogan asked, his tone hopeful.

"That, too."

"Finally, you have some good news for us."

"That is clever," Xuxan marveled. "Sailing in to port, one would never know there was an entire village hidden in the trees."

"Nor would you know you were being watched by sentries," Boone said. "But they are there."

He raised his sword high, giving a signal. Another group of men emerged from the forest, slowly slinking forward and taking positions behind the Albion military. Rogan and Javan's eyes widened when they realized that the new arrivals were Pryten savages. They stared at the sailors intently. Then, anticipating an attack, Rogan began to draw steel, but Boone stopped him.

"They stand with us, Rogan. See? They aren't attacking."

"The Prytens?" Rogan glared at them in confusion. "By Wodan, man! I told you, a group of them crewed the ship that Karza, brother of the usurper, attacked us with across the ocean! They are aligned with Karac!"

Boone stepped in front of Rogan, wrestling with his sword arm. "Rogan, please! Listen to me. Perhaps there were Prytens serving under Karac's brother, but if so, then they were privateers. The queen has struck an alliance with us."

Rogan stood panting, his posture stiff. He eyed the Prytens with suspicion and loathing, and then turned to Boone.

"Allying themselves with you Albion regulars? The world has truly gone insane."

"Karac is a mighty warrior and a devious one, my lord," Boone explained. "He slew all the Captains of the guard with assassins disguised as slaves before the revolution started. As I said, I was far off—lucky to be hunting with Teran. That's how I avoided the blade meant for me. Some of the other elite guards escaped, as well. Many of us are scattered around Albion, plotting revenge, trying to avoid the spells of the usurper's wizard. We need allies, and we take them where we find them—even if they are Prytens. If I may, Rogan, you need allies, as well. And so do your kin."

"My brother speaks the truth, sire," Javan agreed. "It is said that politics and war make for strange pillow-mates."

"I don't plan on bedding them," Rogan growled. "Boone, what news of Rohain and Teran?"

"Teran is safe, and part of the fight. Rohain is being held prisoner in the dungeon of the usurper."

"And no one has freed him?"

"Messengers said that forces are gathered in Cramond with many of the surviving elite troopers. They have struck a bargain to use Cramonds and Thulish barbarian warriors in an attack on Karac ... with Thyssen.

"Then the old goat survives?" Rogan laughed.

Boone grinned. "Yes, sire. I fear he plots a dangerous course for an invasion. To speak honestly, it is one I'm not keen on."

"Explain."

"Karac's magic returned your daughter, Erin, to him. He plans to mate her on the sign day of Damballah. I've heard that—"

He trailed off as Rogan stomped away, pushing past the soldiers and Prytens, and vent his rage on the nearest tree trunk. The assembled men watched in stunned, silent amazement as the hulking gray barbarian reduced the tree to splinters in a matter of minutes. Only then, breathing heavy and dripping with sweat, did he return to Boone.

"You were saying?"

Boone swallowed hard. "Karac trusts no one. He is suspicious of everyone ... even of his wizard, Papa Bon Deux. He feels the earth under him and listens to his guts, from what they say. He offered Thyssen the generalship of his forces, and ..."

"And your father spat in his eye?"

"No." Boone shook his head. "The old man flinched."

Rogan brooded, staring at the Prytens and how well armed they were ... then at the female figure emerging from their guard.

"My king," Boone said, "I beg your apology for delivering such bad news. But I'll say again, it is good to see you, sire. We stand ready to fight for you."

Rogan kept his eyes on Boone and the growing host of red-haired Pryten warriors behind him. "I am not king, Boone. Not anymore. I keep reminding your brother of that, as well."

"He does," Javan agreed quietly.

"Rohain is king now," Rogan insisted. "That life was naught for me. You and your men fight for him, as will I."

"We all will die for you," Boone proclaimed, raising his sword high over his head.

The force of warriors confirmed his declaration with a mighty roar. Swords clanged and flashed in the sunlight. A frightened flock of birds burst from the treetops, squawking as they took flight. The chickens darted down the beach, searching for a calmer area.

"The King of Thule has unleashed his horde," Boone said. "He wants blood for the life of his daughter, Darva, Rohain's queen."

Rogan closed his eyes, recalling the images of his daughter in law, slain in sacrifice—and her baby, his grandson, dying as well.

Boone pointed to the assembled ranks. "Ready or not, they cannot be quelled. We only have so much time before they assault Albion in full. These men of the Prytens have joined with us for a cost."

Rogan eyed the woman from amongst the savages. "This is their queen?"

"Aye," Boone confirmed.

"That is not Queen Tancorix," Rogan said, some disappointment and doubt in his voice.

Before Boone could respond, Xuxan informed Rogan that he needed to begin the unloading process. The captain hurried back to the ship. Rogan stalked away, standing alone, and poking at the sand with the tip of his sword.

"Should we go to him?" Boone asked.

"Nay," answered Javan. "He is in one of his moods. Better to let him brood. He'll rejoin us soon enough. Come, and I will introduce you to Zenata. In her tongue, her name means gift of God. I should warn you—she only has one breast. It is the way of her people. But you would do well not to dwell on it, lest she take offense."

"Is she easily offended?"

"No. She is good-humored and intelligent, and one of the fiercest warriors I have ever known. And I have told her of you."

"Did you warn her that I'm better looking?"

Laughing, the two brothers hustled toward the ship. The

soldiers and the Prytens assisted in the offloading. The sailors from Olmek-Tikal moved about them warily at first, distrustful of these new arrivals. The Kennebeck natives, being so far from home, stared at the beach and forest with wonder.

Rogan was still brooding when Akibeel approached him, staggering slowly across the sand.

"What do you want, shaman?" Rogan grunted. "I am not in the mood."

"Rogan, is it wise to let word spread that you are back in Albion?"

"What do you mean?"

"These men plan to die for you. Is not your bastard son, Karac, to be king?"

"Let him know I am here. Perhaps he will be fearful, and make a mistake."

"Captain Xuxan says your other son is being held in his dungeon. Might not Karac kill him upon hearing this news?"

Rogan gripped the side of his head. "Damn me forever for becoming a bitch to these politicians. I have not the head for such maneuvering. I should've stayed a pirate!"

The young Pryten woman glided toward them. As she approached, she shed her over-cloak, revealing a mane of long, black tresses that hung to the waist. Akibeel wheezed as she threw back her hair. Her breasts were hardly in check by the few straps of leather crossing them. Her private areas were barely obscured in the same fashion by a buckskin skirt. Though sensual in her manner of walking, her body was almost boyish and muscular as she took up a stance, hands on her hips, to face the former King of Albion. A slender blade hung sheathed at her left hip, and two daggers were clipped onto her small waist belt. The hilt of another stuck from the top of her leather boots. Though her hair was obsidian, her eyelashes looked auburn in color ... and unlike the other Prytens, her eyes were blue, not black.

"You should introduce her to me," Akibeel whispered.

"You are not Tancorix," Rogan muttered, ignoring the old man. "How do you come here to us at such a landing?"

"Tancorix is ashes," the girl said, staring at Rogan intensely. "You are disappointed?"

"I knew Tancorix," Rogan admitted. "And you are the queen of the Prytens now? The one they call Andraste? They say you are her daughter. I see it in you."

Ignoring his question, she turned to Akibeel. "You can see things from afar?"

Akibeel nodded.

"So can I," she said. "The magic of the Druids showed me of your peril, Rogan, both in Albion and in the land beyond the sea."

"You come here with the rebels to aid me against Karac?" Rogan snorted dubiously. "Since when do the Prytens support those in Albion for anything other than a hefty price?"

"Nothing has changed." The girl grinned. "My mother showed you that long ago, you picked the wrong side when you chose clean, safe, modern Albion over the Prytens in the war. You should have stayed true to your nature. There are things greater than wealth, gold, or comfort."

"Your mother?" Rogan's eyes narrowed. "Name yourself, girl."

"Very well." She performed a half-curtsy, half-bow, and then stood up again, smiling. "I am, as you guessed, Andraste, queen of the Prytens, daughter of the warrior queen, Tancorix, whom you rutted with. Indeed, I was the product of your coupling."

Akibeel gasped. "Then that means ..."

"Wodan," Rogan whispered.

Andraste's smile faded. "Hello, father."

CHAPTER 3
STRANGE BEDFELLOWS

After leaving behind a group of Kennebeck warriors and Olmek-Tikal sailors to guard the ship, Rogan, Javan, Akibeel, Zenata, Xuxan, and the rest of the crew followed the group of soldiers and savages deep into the grim Pryten wilderness, heading toward the real Monas. Boone and the strutting queen of the Prytens led the procession, followed by the Prytens, and then the outcast military, and finally Rogan's party. The trees loomed over them, seeming to press together everywhere except for the winding footpath, wide enough for three men to walk side by side and bare of everything except for fallen leaves and jutting roots. They occasionally passed by camouflaged hunting blinds and tree-stands, and each time, a Pryten would peel off from the procession and resume sentry duty.

Soon, the sky was a distant memory as the sun was blackened out by the primal forest. No torches were lit, although the day had seemingly turned to night. As their eyes adjusted, the new arrivals noticed that the path was marked on each side with white, glowing lines.

"What sorcery is that?" Xuxan mused.

"It is not magic," Javan explained. "Instead, I suspect it is limestone, crushed up into a powder and used to light the way."

He knelt and touched one of the lines with the tip of his index finger. Then he tasted it, and wiped the residue on his clothing.

"Was it limestone?" Zenata asked.

Javan nodded, grimacing. "Yes. And I do not enjoy the taste. I much prefer the taste of you."

Giggling, Zenata blushed. A second later, realizing that the others had heard him, Javan followed suit.

Rogan shook his head. "I liked it better when both of you were behaving like hardened warriors, rather than lovesick children."

"Ignore our gray-haired friend," Akibeel told Zenata. "I believe he might be jealous. Perhaps his wood lacks its former girth and glory."

Rogan glared at the shaman. "I can still get hard enough to fuck your eyes right out of their sockets, you toothless old—"

"Come along," Boone called from up ahead. "We still have a way to go."

Eventually the path widened into a large clearing. It had started as a natural hollow amidst the forest, but the surrounding hillsides had been cleared of trees and brush, and were now covered with buildings, huts, and tents. This then, was the real Monas. In the center of the village, straddling a creek that wound between the slopes, was a grand lodge, with a roof designed to dissipate camp-fire smoke before it reached the treetops, thus hiding the village's location from prying eyes off the coastline. Gardens bloomed in the sunlight. The smell of roasting meat filled the air. Unlike the fake port on the shore, Monas bustled with activity. Livestock squawked and mooed from crude pens. Pryten children played and shouted, chasing each other and pretending to be warriors. Men and women hurried back and forth, attending to various tasks, but stopping to stare with suspicion at the new arrivals. It was also evident that those from Albion kept separate from the rough, dirty Pryten savages. They headed to their own line of tents, erected at one edge of the village.

As the procession spread out, and the Prytens and Albion soldiers scattered, Rogan nodded at Akibeel and Zenata to go on, and drew Javan aside. Xuxan stayed close to them, eyeing the villagers with suspicion.

"You do not trust them," Rogan said to the captain.

"No," Xuxan confirmed. "I do not."

"Good." Rogan turned to Javan. "Does it strike you as odd that your half-brother has thrown with this lot?"

"Desperate times, sire," Javan replied curtly, his eyes following Zenata. "Need I remind you that the last time you desired to preserve Albion, you did so with the vaunted Queen Tancorix?"

"No, you need not."

"And now here we are." Javan gestured across the clearing at Andraste, who was watching them intently. "Yet another example of what you will do to preserve your desires."

Rogan slammed a forearm into Javan, knocking him askew. Quickly, the smaller man righted himself beside the barbarian.

"Surviving Queen Tancorix's embrace," Rogan muttered, "was nearly as challenging as the foes we faced then."

Javan raised an eyebrow. "And the foes we face now are any different? My point is this, uncle. You have a habit of leaving feral, bastard children in the world. Perhaps that is a good thing this day? If Boone speaks the truth, then they can aid us against your other bastard son."

Xuxan nodded over at Andraste. "That is another of your children?"

"So she says." Rogan shrugged. "If she is indeed from the womb of fabled Queen Tancorix, I hold no ticket as the only man to conquer that slit. She resembles her mother in form, but I do not see my likeness in her."

"I do," Javan said.

Instead of responding, Rogan stalked toward Boone and Andraste, who stood near the grand lodge. After a moment, Javan followed after him, while Xuxan saw to his men.

"There are hundreds of troopers scattered in this wilderness,"

Boone said to Rogan as they approached, "but this is our only permanent camp, and we could strike it or torch it in a half day, should the need arise. The wizard of Karac, Papa Bon Deux, has minions and eyes in the sky. What you see here is just a small part of our might. If we concentrate our forces ..."

"They could slaughter us in one fell swoop," Rogan murmured, "and darkness will fall forever."

"Aye."

Satisfied that his crew were being cared for and fed, Xuxan rejoined them. After a moment, so did Akibeel and Zenata.

"These Pryten women are like animals," Akibeel observed. "Except for that queen."

Rogan turned as Andraste strutted over and took a drink from a shabby skin of liquid. She drained it, wiped her mouth with the back of her hand, and then stabbed her fingers at four of her subjects.

"Bring the seer and the portal. I shall dine on your balls this evening if you do not hurry."

Nodding and bowing, the four men swiftly scuttled toward a nearby hut.

Javan leaned near Xuxan and whispered, "She certainly sounds like Rogan."

The captain covered his mouth with his hand, suppressing a laugh.

Waving his large hands out as if he was embracing the scattered crowd, Rogan asked Boone, "How many men do you have, total, throughout the land?"

Boone frowned. "That is hard to say for sure. The regular military of Albion stays scattered in this forest along with the elite troopers. They take turns bunking here in the village. Who knows how many savages Queen Andraste has at her disposal? Thousands perhaps."

"You haven't asked her?"

"She is ... difficult, my lord."

Xuxan leaned close to Javan and Zenata. "That sounds like Rogan, too."

Boone continued, "I know that a few thousand of the troops loyal to Rohain are camped north of Albion, awaiting forces from Cramond and beyond. Many of those Thule troops will be berserk fighters, but they can fight and die as easy as anyone else."

Andraste raised her husky voice and pointed at Rogan. "We will dine soon, but first, come and see, father dearest."

Her tone dripped with sarcasm, and her smile was mischievous, as if her venom swam thin.

"We would eat now," Rogan replied. "We have traveled far, and lived off sea fare for too long."

"First, let us answer your questions. I will show you the true options, better than these men with their military minds and well-trained hearts. I will reveal it to you using Pryten magic."

Akibeel perked to attention. "I would see this, as well, Rogan."

"Of course," Andraste complied. "All of my father's inner circle is welcome to watch. But be warned—the rites are not for the weak of heart or stomach."

"Then you don't know this group well," Rogan muttered.

Flanked by two guards on either side of the door, Andraste pulled back a leather flap and motioned at the group to enter the lodge. Boone went first, followed closely by Akibeel, Zenata, Javan and Xuxan. Rogan paused in front of Andraste, as more Prytens gathered around.

"You speak of me as your forbearer with confidence, girl."

Andraste's nostrils flared. "I am a woman, father. You would do well to acknowledge that. You may find, before this war is done, that a woman is what you need, instead of those who call themselves men."

She turned briskly and disappeared into the lodge. Rogan hesitated for a moment, eyeing the guards. Then, he followed after her. The flap fell shut behind him, and he was surrounded by darkness. He waited for his eyes to adjust. A small orange flame flickered in the center of the blackness. Slowly, the rest of his party came into view, seated around it. He had just walked over and joined them, when the flap opened again. Two lean Prytens entered, bearing up a short, obese man with milky white skin. He gibbered and begged as they dragged him across the floor. Just before the door closed again, Rogan spotted another figure entering the lodge. This curious arrival looked almost like a walking, man-sized tree, but melted into the darkness so quickly that it became invisible.

"On your guard," Rogan whispered to Javan and Zenata.

"I saw it, too," Zenata said.

The Prytens dragged the man over to the assembly. He flopped about in their grip, sputtering. Tears stained his chubby cheeks. Rogan raised an eyebrow, knowing this man was obviously kidnapped from the surrounding territory of Albion. His complexion, silken clothing, and dialect—which was crisp and to the point—were not native of this wilderness.

"Unhand me, vile savages," the man cried. His tone was resilient, as if he expected the Pryten's to obey him.

Andraste laughed. "Do as he says."

The Prytens dropped the fat man to his buttocks and knelt on his arms, pinning him down. Two more savages scrambled out of the shadows and secured his legs. The eyes of the fat man focused on Rogan, then widened with recognition

"It is the king," he gasped. "By the goddess! I am saved! Sire, I beg of you, tell these fools to unhand me!"

Rogan looked at Andraste, who lolled her body back on her right hip. Her hands were on her waist and her eyes danced. Then he turned his attention back to the man.

"From where in Albion do you hail?"

Confused that the king had not immediately ordered his release, the man stammered at first. "F-from the western banks of the Severn River, my lord. Near the wilderness. My family has made finery for the ladies of Albion for many generations."

"A dressmaker?" Rogan's tone was dubious. "And you were foolish enough to be taken prisoner by these men?"

"What do you mean?" the fat man squawked. "They came unto my home, broke in the doors and stole me like a common trollop!"

"A trollop would be more useful," Boone muttered.

Xuxan nodded. "Probably would have smaller tits, though."

Shooting them a stern look, Rogan returned his gaze to the man. "But all the years of the past, you were not molested by the Prytens."

Gasping for air, the man admitted, "Nay, sire. Not once. We saw them from afar at night, burning their fires to their pagan gods, but no, they never molested us or came out of the forest. We never even saw one ... but we could smell them on the wind."

Rogan scratched his nose and leaned over to glower at the fat man. "I wonder why they never attacked you before?"

The fat man replied steadily, "Why, they knew that the revenge of the king would be so severe, that it wasn't worth the trouble."

"Who is king of Albion?" Rogan asked him.

The man opened his mouth to speak, but only sighed.

"Out with it," Rogan grumbled. "Who is the king of Albion? Who is it that cannot hold the savages at bay?

"King Karac," the dressmaker moaned.

Rogan leapt to his feet, causing the Pryten captors to scatter. Although freed, the fat man could only cower as the barbarian towered over him.

"You dare speak the name of the vile usurper unto me, fat dog?"

A stench filled the lodge as the trembling prisoner urinated on himself.

"Rohain was deposed," he sobbed. "I meant no offense. Karac is your son, King Rogan."

"And you thought one boy from my balls was good as another, aye?"

The man almost shrugged, but then appeared to think better of it.

Rogan spat on him. "Then ask Karac to wrap you in his protective arms. What puzzles me is what use the Prytens have for one such as you?"

Andraste smiled, teeth flashing in the darkness. "Come forward now, Weaver."

A willowy figure emerged from the shadows and glided toward them with a scraping sound. Rogan was unsure if tree branches or deer antlers grew from the head of this muddy individual ... or indeed, if it was a man or a woman. His pulse quickened at the thought of necromancy. The stench wafting off the figure was revolting.

Andraste snapped her fingers, and the Prytens seized the dressmaker again, holding him prone on the floor.

Weaver stopped, tilted its head, and stared down at the fat man. The prisoner yelped. His captors trembled, even as they pinned him. Swaying slowly back and forth, Weaver made no sound, but Rogan heard leaves rustling. His breath came quickly, and he was surprised to discover that even he had fallen back from this ominous presence.

And then ... Weaver spoke, with a creaky voice that sounded like the wind in the branches.

"Open."

Lightning fast, another Pryten appeared, wielding a sharp battle-axe. Even in the dim light, Rogan could tell by the craftsmanship that the weapon had been forged in Albion—probably plundered or stolen during a raid. With a grunt, the savage swung the axe down over the body of the dressmaker, planting it in his lower abdomen. Blood splattered his captor's faces and arms. The fat man's screams turned to shrieks.

"Open wider," Weaver said.

The axe slid back, gouging a huge crevasse in the captive's large stomach. His intestines uncurled from his girth like writhing, purplish-white snakes.

Akibeel staggered forward, leaning against Rogan for support, and watched with obvious fascination as the fat man struggled with death. Weaver knelt, gripped a coil of guts, and looked at

Akibeel with dark eyes. Rogan glanced at each of them, convinced that some bizarre, silent communion was taking place between the wizards.

"Come, Rogan." Weaver beckoned. "See what is your kingdom."

Rogan hesitated. Weaver nodded, and waved the fistful of steaming intestines. Rogan grimaced. Akibeel gently nudged him.

"Lean forward," the shaman whispered. "Breathe deeply. I shall be there with you. As will Javan."

"You know my thoughts on magic," Rogan muttered. "I don't trust this ... thing."

"But you trust me. I will guard your back."

"And we shall guard his," Javan promised.

Sighing, Rogan gave a curt nod. Then he leaned forward on his haunches and addressed Weaver. "If this is a trick, I will snap you the way a hurricane snaps a tree."

"Relax," Weaver answered, "and breeeeeeathe ..."

ROGAN BEHOLDS A PAINTING WITHIN THE WARM, STINKING INNARDS. His eyes widen as the lone painting splinters into many paintings that move like a living dream. He sees the cultured nobles of Albion walking with their heads down, their vibrant clothes dim, cutting their arms to give blood droplets at street corners to small idols of the bat god, Damballah, erected by the new king.

He sees the young girls of his land all separated from their families, their womanhood mutilated, their clitorises cut free and put in jars filled with preserving fluid. Rogan shudders, seething with rage and disgust. The jars are given to the wizards of Karac, who gloat over them, rubbing the surfaces with glee. The girls are singed to heal and then turned over to the king's warriors to serve as vessels. Their parents, if they object, join the avenue of the crucified that serve as a rotting, foul lesson to any who would rise up against Karac.

Rogan tries to scream, and finds that he cannot. He has never felt more helpless or impotent than he does at this moment. He feels his gorge rise until he thinks he will choke on it.

"Remember," he hears Akibeel say. "I am here. I watch your back while Javan watches mine. These are just visions. They are real, but they are smoke."

Groaning, Rogan clenches his teeth and focuses on Karac's warlock. His name is Papa Bon Deux, and he is a man of some girth. He is clad in a baggy kilt, wears no shirt, and has a hat like a stove chimney perched askew on his head. He draws incantations to the dark snake god of his homeland, and pisses into the well of the temple of the pure goddess, and laughs at the cries of Albion's people. His laughter is echoed by the teetering cackling of a female wizard—a dark crone dressed in a floor length dress and a feathered hat.

Rogan's moans increase. He begins to shake.

"No more," Akibeel urges. "The connection is killing him."

"No," Rogan gasps, choking on his gorge. "I need ... to ... see ..."

The laughter grows louder, overpowering them.

SHUDDERING, ROGAN OPENED HIS EYES. HE LEANED BACK, gasping and bathed in sweat. Akibeel patted his shoulder, murmuring in assurance, until Rogan angrily pushed him away.

"Uncle?" Javan inched closer. "Are you okay?"

Rogan waved at him. Stomach acid burned his throat.

"I'm fine," he croaked.

"What did you see?" Boone asked.

"What did I see?" Rogan stood up, wheeling angrily on the assembly. "I'll tell you what I didn't see. The face of my son. I saw the suffering faces of the people of Albion. I saw the leering face of that monster, Papa Bon Deux. I see your faces. I see the face of this fat fucking dressmaker. But nowhere did I see the face of my son. For all of this tree-thing's magic, for all of Akibeel's words, I see not the face of Rohain. If he is dead or rotten, let it be clear to me."

"He lives," Weaver murmured, "but his image is too dark for me to find."

"Akibeel tells me the same thing." Rogan snorted. "Bah, what use are your kind?"

The old Kennebeck shaman flinched, and then stared helplessly at the floor.

Rogan turned to face Queen Andraste. "You have your creature show me this for what? What perverse pleasure do you get from throwing all this in my face?"

Andraste mock-feigned a surprised look of innocence. "I just show you the truth, great King Rogan."

Rogan spat on the floor. "And it gets you wet to see fair Albion turning from its bright gods and civilized ways to a darker path?"

Andraste shrugged. "It makes me wonder why you want to save it."

Rogan rocked back on his heels. "What?"

Zenata stirred, hand slipping to her dagger hilt, but Javan grabbed her wrist and shook his head in warning.

"For a civilized populace," Andraste continued, "the people of Albion have certainly come to embrace a darker way, worse far than that of the Prytens, with open arms. This is the land you want to save? The people you wish to deliver? Why? To switch it back so they can plot for the next usurper of the throne? Maybe it will be another bastard from your loins. Perhaps he will worship bulls and make them all try to breed with cattle. And do you know what, father? They will comply. They will rut with cattle in the street if commanded to do so. Your kingdom's population are sheep."

Boone jumped to his feet. "What else is there for us to do? Rogan must lead us into Albion, slay that bastard on the throne, and save his son ... save his children."

Smiling, Andraste rose and walked over to Rogan, nudging Javan, Zenata, and Akibeel aside. Zenata glared at the queen, but held her tongue.

"There is another option, father," Andraste whispered.

"Aye," Xuxan snorted. "He can get back on my boat and go

back to Olmek-Tikal, forgetting about all of this. He can go fishing."

"I could," Rogan agreed.

"But you won't." Andraste's long fingernails grazed his rough chest. "There is a beast in you, father, but it does not live in your heart. You could walk away from your other children, but your heart would never let you forget. You can't drink or fuck or fight it out of yourself. I know what must be done."

"To Albion?" Rogan chuckled. "What is that? What is your other option?"

She grinned. "Destruction. That is the way of the Kelt, is it not? I heard that you led a force of Kelts and exterminated every life in fabled Kemet. Every man, woman, and child. You even killed their livestock."

"I was a boy then, barely a man. Slaying all of those lives under that Pharaoh was a pleasure."

"And what was the name of that ruler in Kemet?"

Now Rogan grinned. "I will not speak it, nor will anyone ever again. His name is blotted out forever and so is that of his children, whom I slew, one by one, all one hundred and fifty of them."

"Then you should do the same for Karac," Andraste said, "so that no one ever recalls him."

Rogan's smile faded. "I cannot slay an entire realm for the sake of a usurper."

"Extermination works, dear father," Andraste giggled. "Every time it is tried."

"And what will I enact this genocide with?" Rogan asked. "What force? These ragtag folks? The remnants of Boone's army? A group of berserk Thulists? A few pissed off Cramonds in kilts, hiding out in the wilderness? These Kennebeck braves and sailors from Olmek-Tikal against loyalists and traitors in Albion ... well-armed and trained, plus whatever force of savages Karac has marching here? You are deluded, little girl, and fooling yourself."

"It is you who are deluded, big man." Her smile slipped and her eyes flashed with fury. "My warriors are all around us. And I have other forces you have yet to meet."

Rogan glanced at Boone. "What does she speak of?"

"I know not, sire."

"Weaver," Andraste said. "Go outside and call them."

The mysterious sorcerer nodded, and then glided out of the lodge.

"Come." Andraste beckoned them. "I will show you all what I am speaking of."

They exited the lodge and followed the queen toward the edge of the village. When they reached the tree line, Andraste spread her arms out as if to embrace the forest. As she did this, the bark on the ancient trees seemed to shake off. Rogan and the others drew steel as figures clambered down from the treetops. Scurrying down the trunks and swinging off the limbs were simian-like creatures that moved like apes, but sported humanoid faces. These beasts all carried knives in their teeth and hunched over toward the earth once they were on the ground. More trees rustled in the distance as a further horde dropped to the forest floor. Rogan was stunned by their number. He relaxed, realizing they weren't attacking.

"What are they?" Boone asked.

"Perhaps they are what we once were," Andraste purred. "They are relics from a bygone time. They are one with nature, not quite human, and yet, not animal. They are Troglodytes. Loyal to me, to a fault. They will die for me and my desires."

Boone gaped at the assembled forces. "And in all the time we've been here among your people, why am I just learning of them now?"

Andraste smiled at him. "A girl must keep some secrets."

"How many are there?" Javan questioned.

She turned to him, appraising his form openly. Zenata bristled, but Rogan shook his head at her.

"A valid question." Andraste pursed her lips and arched her hips. "How many trees are there?"

Javan frowned. "That is no answer, ma'am."

Her eyes widened. "Ma'am? Oh, this one is priceless, father."

"That is one word for Javan," Rogan replied.

Andraste sidled up to Javan and said, "That is one reason why he is my desire."

The group glanced at each other, confused. Zenata stepped forward, placing herself between the queen and Javan. The Troglodytes and the Prytens both grew tense, sensing confrontation.

"Stay your hand, Zenata," Rogan ordered. "What do you mean, Andraste? What game are you playing?"

"Easy," Andraste answered. "You think I will comply with you because your blood runs in my veins. You believe that I will help you in any regard? Bah! That is not the way of blood, is it, father?"

"It is, but you are not of my folk, girl. You may share my blood, but you are not one of us."

She stared at Javan as she spoke. "True. I am a Pryten. And I desire a mating—a proper one. That is the way of my folk. You know all too well, father. You still bear the scars from your mating with my mother. And this man here, this nephew of yours; he will serve the purpose I desire."

"Then you will die before you get it," Zenata snarled.

In response, the agitated Troglodytes began to hoot and growl. The Prytens raised their weapons. Rogan's party returned the gesture.

"No." Javan gripped Zenata's arm and turned her toward him. He lifted her chin and stared into her eyes for a long moment. Then he stepped forward, inches from his would-be suitor.

Andraste raised an eyebrow. "Young man, you are not afraid of the prospect?"

Studious as ever, Javan replied, "One must face death every day, ma'am."

Boone stepped forward and puffed up his burly chest. "Javan is a boy, hardly a man. I am his better in every matter. It is I who should bed her, Rogan. I could live through it and live to fight another day."

Andraste shook her head. "No. I want the boy."

"Why?" Rogan asked

"Because." She grinned and gestured at Boone. "He wishes it not to be so."

"This is petty crap," Boone argued. "She holds us hostage over her carnal lust?"

"Calm yourself," Rogan warned. "Kingdoms have been slain for worse. I've fought a war for beer and pussy before. It happens."

"No, it doesn't," Zenata said, preparing to throw herself at the queen.

Before she could act, Rogan nodded at Xuxan. The captain barked an order, and several sailors restrained the enraged warrior woman. She fought with them, but more rushed forward, holding her arms.

"Do not fight," Javan told her, his voice calm. "It will be okay."

Rogan placed his big hand on Javan's shoulder. "Nephew?"

"Yes, sire?"

"My future is in the palm of your hands, or between your legs, as it were. Are you certain about this? You understand bedding her will be unlike anything you are accustomed to?"

"We all have a part to play," Javan answered steadfastly. "I do this for Rohain and for Albion. And for you, uncle."

"Very well." Rogan nodded. "Don't fail me."

Javan eyed Andraste. "I will do my best, sire."

Andraste took Javan by the hand and led him into the forest. The Troglodytes parted like a field of corn swaying in the wind, allowing them passage. No one spoke, save for Zenata, who yelled and thrashed, breaking one of her captor's arms. She was about to gut another before Akibeel stopped her, attempting to soothe the distraught girl.

Rogan eyed one of the Prytens. "Your queen promised us food."

They were led to a long, wooden table set in the open air. It was lined with food and drink, and most of Xuxan's crew sat around it. The others joined them. Xuxan snatched up a wooden goblet and drank. Akibeel declined to sit, declaring that he was tired, and was shown to a tent.

Rogan sat on a tree stump apart from the others, drinking wine and goat's milk, and eating beef and fruit and a mash made of grains. He watched the sailors from Olmek-Tikal and the Kennebeck warriors laughing like old friends, and mused on how fate had brought them together. Then he saw Zenata, weeping inconsolably among the sailors. He raised a cup and caught Xuxan's attention. The captain hurried over to him.

"Yes, Rogan?"

"Are your crew and the Kennebeck folk cared for?"

Xuxan nodded. "Our hosts were true to their word."

Rogan nodded at Zenata. "Keep an eye on her. I'd not have your men taking advantage of her grief."

"She's already broken one of their arms. I pity the fool who attempts any such thing."

"Still," Rogan replied. "Be mindful. Hopefully Javan will return to us. If he doesn't, I fear what Zenata will do. We can't have her passions—no matter how just she thinks they may be—ruin what is afoot."

Xuxan nodded. "Understood. I will watch over her as if she were my own daughter. But Rogan ...?"

Rogan raised his head up and met his glance. "Yes?"

"Surely, your nephew will return. It's just two people rutting."

"It's nothing like that at all," Rogan said, and then lowered his head and returned to his meal.

Xuxan returned to his seat at the table. Rogan looked up to shout for more wine, and saw Boone walking in circles.

"Boone," the aged barbarian hollered, "come sit down before I knock you down."

Boone stumbled over to him. His expression was slack.

"What ails you, Boone?"

Boone seemed surprised. "Javan ..."

"Javan will do or die," Rogan muttered and looked at the weeping girl. "There, that is what love will get you. Each and every time. I am very proud of Javan, even if Andraste breaks his prick off and Zenata cries herself to dust. Javan was not hampered by sentiment or feelings. He acted, doing what was best. He will be a fine man."

CHAPTER 4
THE MANY PATHS TO WAR

R ogan squatted on the stump again, eating a breakfast of cold chicken and even colder porridge. The latter was thick to the consistency of spackle, and clung to his wooden spoon, no matter how much he shook it. Occasionally, he looked up from his meal to see others glancing at him—Prytens, Albion's soldiers, and those who had travelled across the ocean with him. He knew that all of them had taken to referring to the stump as "his new throne," though none save Akibeel and Xuxan had the sack to say it to his face—and they only dared when they were out of range of his fists.

He weighed his options, pondering how best to deal with Karac and rescue his children—and the kingdom he had once ruled. Rogan didn't relish leading this haggard lot off to war, but he didn't see any other choice, short of storming Albion by himself and hacking his way through everyone until he found his bastard son.

Morning mist rose from the ground, curling through the trees. Dew clung to the grass and dripped from the leaves. The air was chilly, but not unpleasant. Doves and whippoorwills called to each other from the treetops. Although still early, the village began to wake. Sailors tromped in from the forest path after guarding the boat overnight, and replacements hiked down the path toward the beach. Soldiers and savages sharpened their weapons after scarfing down meals. The Kennebeck and the rest of Xuxan's crew tossed dice and gambled. There was no sign of Javan or the Pryten queen, nor were Weaver or the Troglodytes to be seen. Apparently, they had melted back into the forest. Rogan spied Zenata, however, moving among the men with confidence and strength. A quick glance at her demeanor and one would think she'd already gotten over her broken heart. But Rogan knew better. The warrior girl's eyes told a much different story.

Akibeel approached him, walking slowly, his joints obviously stiff from the dampness in the air. He didn't ask to join Rogan, nor did Rogan offer. He simply sat quietly, next to the tree stump, crossed his legs, and pulled a small leather bag from his waist. He opened it, shook out a few nuts, and began to nibble at them.

"Hard to eat these the way I used to," he said, after a few minutes. "We take our teeth for granted until we don't have them anymore."

Grunting, Rogan handed the old shaman his half-eaten bowl of porridge.

"Thank you," Akibeel said.

"You're already skin and bones. Can't have you wasting away before this business is done. I might need you yet."

"You're thinking of the sorcerer we saw in the vision?"

"Yes."

"Well, it takes a wizard to kill a wizard."

"Horseshit. Steel works just as well."

They sat there for a long time, watching the village wake up, comfortable in each other's company without having to fill the silence with words.

Finally, after finishing his breakfast, Akibeel spoke again. "Your nephew?"

"No word yet." Rogan stared out at the forest. "And I will speak no more of it. If you must talk, then talk about the weather or something."

Akibeel shrugged. "There's a cool breeze at our backs and on our foreheads this morning."

"Yes," Rogan agreed. "It will be a good day to start the march to Albion."

"Then you have decided?"

Rogan nodded. "It does not sit well with me, but I see no alternative."

Akibeel tottered to his feet. "I will let my people know."

"Inform Xuxan, as well. And if you see Boone, send him to me."

"As you wish." Akibeel performed a mock bow, and almost lost his balance. His eyes went wide with panic, and he dropped the empty wooden bowl. Rogan chuckled as the old man righted himself.

"I still think you'd make a better jester than a shaman, Akibeel, but I have been glad of your company on this trip."

Akibeel opened his mouth to respond, then closed it again. He cocked his head, staring at Rogan intently.

"Yes," Rogan growled. "I said something nice. Now go, before I reconsider it and break your damned spine!"

Rogan waited a while. Boone responded to his summons, and Rogan told him to ready his troops. When Xuxan came to him, he advised the captain of the same, ordering him to leave a conscription of men behind to guard the ship from any pirates or the Prytens not marching to Albion with them.

Eventually, Andraste emerged from the forest, a slight smile on her face. She sidled over to where Rogan sat. He regarded her but briefly, and then pointedly looked away from her.

"I was wondering if you survived," he said.

She snorted laughter. "You'd be proud of your nephew. He lives, as well."

Rogan shrugged. "I expected no less from him. He is every bit as resourceful as my own children."

"Ah, your children. My half-brothers and sisters. Do you care for us all equally?"

Ignoring the question, Rogan finally turned to face her. "Have your filthy people prepare to march. We leave today. And I want your Troglodytes at the rear of the procession. I won't have them mixing among us. It is bad for morale."

"So it is off to war then?"

Rogan nodded.

"You want to see Albion burn, don't you?"

"Why do you say that, girl?"

"Because, as civilized as a monarchy has made you, barbarian lust and blood will always come down to that. You want to punish them. You thirst for vengeance. They have wounded your pride. You want to see them all die for turning on your created peace."

"My desire is not always right," Rogan mused. "I thought the hearth was for me, but not again. What if all of my children are dead? I will not sit on that damned throne again. All I want to do is settle this once and for all, and then leave and find freedom again. I want my sons to come with me, and my daughters ..."

"How many sisters do I have?" Andraste asked.

"Who knows? Every time I think I have a complete accounting of all my offspring, another one seems to pop up, claiming to have sprung from my seed. Where is Javan? You didn't leave him tied out there in the forest, did you?"

"He is washing up in a fresh water spring, and will join us shortly. I give you my word, father. He is fine."

Andraste removed a leather cord from her neck. On this cord hung a tiny glass vial. She offered it to him.

"What's this?

"Inside are some of the ashes of Tancorix. It has been my totem since she died. I give it to you freely now. Carry them with you as a good luck charm, and I pray the omens will follow you from my mother."

Looking at the gift, Rogan said flatly, "Tancorix never loved me."

"But you loved her," Andraste replied. "That is what counts...to you."

Rogan made a fist over the vial. His hands had snapped spines and trees, ripped the throats and hearts from men and beasts, shattered columns and pillars, bent iron bars, and moved stones—but he cradled the vial gently, tenderly, and then tied it around his neck.

THE RAGTAG ARMY BEGAN THEIR MARCH A LITTLE OVER TWO hours later. They spread out their diverse forces, staggering the groups and their movement, in an effort to confuse any spies and also to better withstand a surprise attack. Rogan and Javan walked far ahead of the rest of the throng, followed distantly by Akibeel, Zenata, Boone and the Albion soldiers. They were followed by Andraste and her Pryten savages, who were flanked in turn by the Kennebeck braves and Xuxan and his sailors. Finally, far to the rear of the procession, hidden amongst the trees, came the Troglodytes.

They journeyed all day and made camp in the evening. The forest had begun to thin, giving way here and there to rolling hills and grassland. Rogan ordered the various regiments to camp apart from each other, in the same order they had marched. Then he and Javan walked ahead, hiking to the top of a rocky hill. They stood on a boulder, and Rogan scanned the tree line and the sky as the sun disappeared behind him. Javan stood beside him, not speaking. The boy had two black eyes, a bloodied lip, and scratches all along his limbs and chest. Alone, they looked across the lessening forest that separated them from the lovely green land of Albion.

"What think you of the consul of war a day back?" Rogan asked. "I can believe what you say about trusting these sub-human Troglodytes or her ideas for destruction."

Hands behind his back, Javan said, "I am glad to hear the scattered forces of the Albion army are gathering in the territories around Albion. At the very least, if such an army is getting ready for war, they may encounter this force coming at us from the south, if indeed such a force exists. Karac will surely see this—and us—as well. If that is the case, we will need the Troglodytes."

"True."

"However," Javan continued, "the idea of you and I going ahead of the rest of them, sneaking into the capitol city, and attempting to, shall we say, handle this ourselves ..."

"You would prefer that?"

"Not specifically, sire. Need I remind you of what I did last night to secure this army for you?"

"You agreed willingly, boy."

"I did. I am your servant and will follow your command, whatever my own preference. Nevertheless, I comprehend what your true desire is more than these folk. You don't want war. You want revenge."

Rogan chuckled. "Andraste said something similar this morning."

Javan's countenance darkened at the mention of the Pryten queen's name, but he held his poise and said nothing.

"So, what would our forces back yonder do while you and I forged ahead?" Rogan asked.

"Send men on foot to reconnoiter with the other resistors and armies. Have all of them march simultaneously, so that they arrive to keep order should you and I succeed."

"And avenge our deaths on top of all the others should we fail," Rogan said. "Tell me, Javan, what we would do once in the city?"

"You and I will gain access to the palace ground via the secret tunnels you had installed specifically for escape in case of a seizure. We will enter the castle and find where Karac is. Then, you will kill him without prejudice."

"A simple plan, no?"

"Indeed," Javan agreed.

"And you are right. I would prefer it to all this marching and commanding. Would we take any soldiers with us? Or Akibeel, perhaps?"

"We would move better and faster were it just the two of us."

Rogan stood silently, staring out at the horizon, mulling over his nephew's words. The wind tossed his silver bangs and nuzzled the vial around his neck. Finally, he turned back to his nephew.

"You are correct, Javan. I would much prefer this method. I would much prefer to rely on myself, with you by my side, rather than count on this lot we travel with. Do you think me foolhardy in this?"

"It is as good an idea as any, sire," Javan replied. "You have faced similar odds before. If I may speak personally, I would much rather see myself at your side than those ape-things Andraste has aligned us with. And, should we succeed, it would fend off a full-scale war, and we wouldn't need Andraste's army at all."

"Good," Rogan declared. "Then it is decided. You and I shall leave at once."

"Very good, sire."

"You will be okay to travel? You are sufficiently recovered from your time with Andraste?"

"I will be fine, Rogan. The capitol is two days away by foot. If we move quickly, we can reach the border before dawn. Then, we shall only have to rely on stealth."

"We'll probably encounter sentries before then. They will be good practice. We can wet our blades on them. And then, when it comes down to it, I will kill Karac myself. Cutting the head off will make the rest of the snake die."

"Possibly, sire. At the very least, we will find Rohain after this is done and order will return."

"We should return to the camp, and inform the others."

They climbed off the boulder and walked down the hill. The sun had set and the moon was just a sliver. Rogan had ordered that no campfires be lit, and the countryside was swathed in darkness. Despite that, neither man had trouble finding his way in the gloom.

"Javan?"

"Yes, sire?"

"I am glad to see you well."

The young man smiled. "Able bodied at least, sire."

"Remember, you have the rest of your life to worry on romance and love."

Javan frowned, and Rogan knew the youth was thinking of Zenata.

"I may only have a few days left to live, sire, but thank you for reminding me of my sacrifice."

CHAPTER 5

A SIEGE OF TWO

R ogan and Javan reached the border an hour before dawn. Only after they'd killed the sentries posted at the guardhouse and made their way further inland did they stop to catch their breath. Trembling a bit, Rogan leaned against a stout tree for support, and panted, his massive chest heaving. He'd pulled the hood on his cloak down over his face, but he knew it did little to mask his waning stamina.

"Should we rest here a bit, sire?"

"I'm fine." Rogan waved him off. "It will be your curse, too, someday."

"Time marches for all. Save for the dead. And even they are restless."

Head still down, Rogan replied, "Time is all the dead have. Imagine eternity? That must be a bitch."

"Do you remember the stone circle of Lebbon, sire?"

Rogan nodded. "The one cut so well no one can figure out who the hell made it?"

"The same," Javan confirmed. "They called it a circle, but it is more of an oval, with the line of altars up at the top."

Rogan shrugged. "So?"

"It's a vagina."

"You sound like your half-brother, Boone. He sees pussy in everything."

Javan shook his head. "One thought is that the ancients made it as a symbol of fertility and tribute to Mother Earth."

"Lebbon is a snatch or a tribute to a snatch?" Rogan chuckled.

"Do you remember the vast graveyard next to the circle, and how the mists crawled across the stones?"

"Aye, I remember it well. There was always a light fog there."

"It wasn't a fog, sire. They were spirits."

"Spirits?" Rogan sounded skeptical.

"We learned about it in university," Javan explained, "but then I saw it for myself. There are shapes and forms in the fog. They dance about and no one notices, because the townspeople have become accustomed to it."

"Well, fuck me running."

"Aye, the spirits do that, too."

"They fuck?"

"They go through the motions of it, at least. Perhaps it is merely a memory of what they did before."

Rogan frowned. "Spirits screwing one another in the graveyard by the edge of the circle? That's almost as bad as the living fucking each other in the same location."

"I wouldn't think you had any morals about copulating in a graveyard."

"Well, not by choice," Rogan said. "You Albion people are screwy, burying bodies. Why keep those corpses around? That is why my tribe burned the dead, to release the spirit and be one again with the gods. Keeping them around in the ground with a remembrance? Talk about morbid shit."

Javan smiled. "That particular practice is founded on the belief that if one conceives a baby while doing it atop a grave, one will be reincarnated of the warrior or wise man buried below."

"Then if we die here in Albion, make sure my body is burned. I don't want any of these weird bastards fucking on top of my grave.

Better to take your lover to the potter's field and be reincarnated as the piss-pot boy or the maid who washes the cum from the sheets."

Javan shook his head.

"Perhaps that is why the spirits are so restless," Rogan teased. "They don't like being rolled over and screwed in the night."

Javan rolled his eyes "Where are the ogres and wandering monsters when one needs them?"

"We should be so lucky." Rogan adjusted his hood, hiding his face, and drew his cloak tight to better conceal his armor and weapons. "Come now. Enough talk. Let us press on."

They journeyed across the country, pausing only to catch a brief few hours of sleep in an abandoned barn. They stuck to the woodland trails and backroads, avoiding people whenever possible, and as a result, refrained from having to kill anyone save for an unlucky sentry, who challenged them and recognized Rogan.

"How long do you think it will take for our messengers to reach the other rebels?" Rogan inquired as they hiked.

"It depends, sire. Some of them may have already done so, and those troops are probably mustering as we speak. Others are far off. It may take some time for the news to reach them."

"It will reach Karac, as well."

Javan nodded in agreement.

"Then, we reach him first," Rogan declared. "Still, the more I think about it, the gladder I am that we decided on this. Once we kill this bastard, it will be good to have the troops come swooping down to keep order."

"Sire, if I didn't know better, I'd say you still care for the citizenry."

"Bah. I care for my children. I'd not rescue them from the grips of this madman only to see them killed in some resulting uprising or rebellion of noblemen and commoners. Though I can't imagine any commoner will be upset at losing such a cruel overlord. The things Karac is doing ... they turn even my stomach."

Eventually, at sundown on the second day, they reached the outskirts of the capitol city of Albion. The conditions within were shocking. Soldiers from Zimbabwe, loyalist to Karac, patrolled the streets, and a pall seemed to hold sway over all. There was no music or dancing, no laughter or singing, no gambling or carousing nor even fucking. Instead, the city echoed with a grim, almost palpable silence.

They slunk down alleys, clambered over walls and rooftops, and crawled through gardens and pig troughs until they reached a blacksmith's shop. In the rear of the property was a hut disguised as a small privy. Inside, they found an entrance to one of the many escape tunnels. They crouched together, peering into the murky darkness. A rickety wooden ladder led down into the depths below. The sound of water dripping echoed up to them, followed by the squeak of a rat.

"It was nice of the smithy to keep such a thing for you," Javan said.

"This smithy was a good man" Rogan agreed. "One I brought with me from my homeland. His work with metals was amazing."

"You speak of him in past tense?"

Rogan glanced out of the privy door. "He doesn't seem to be about."

"Perhaps ..." Javan started to say, and then stopped himself.

Rogan rummaged around in the back of the hut and moved a moldering old woolen blanket. Beneath it was a plain wooden chest. He undid the hasp and opened it. The hinges creaked and dust filled the cramped space.

"Ah," he whispered. "Good. He still kept them here."

He removed two lanterns and struck the flints. As they began to glow, he glowered at Javan.

"You were going to suggest that perhaps he died in the overthrow?"

Javan shrugged.

Rogan shined a lantern down the hole. "You go first, smart ass."

Sighing, Javan adjusted his bow to climb down the shaft. "It isn't being contrary to point out facts."

"Even if something is true, it doesn't make the ears feel fine. Despite what you may think, I can feel guilt."

Javan accepted one of the lanterns and began his descent. When he was safely at the bottom, Rogan followed after, squeezing his bulk into the tight shaft. The wooden rungs were damp and slimy. He silently cursed his advisors, remembering that, at the time of its installation, they had balked at paying for a metal ladder instead. When he reached the bottom, he wiped the dampness from his hands while Javan brushed cobwebs from his hair. Then, the two ventured into the tunnel. Both men crouched as they moved along. Rogan's head constantly brushed the ceiling.

"I've never been down here," Javan said. "I knew of its construction, as did the others on the council, but I never had need to visit."

"You think I hung out here a lot? I did see it and walk it once, years ago, just after its completion."

"It is a wonder it isn't dank or full of the elements."

Rogan stomped his boot a little. "I had the innards coated with pitch, and gravel set down. I'd of had it paved but I wasn't that damned paranoid of a use for it. It keeps out the water and sewage. Can't say the same for the spiders—or the rats, judging by the sound. I just wish we'd paid for a metal ladder, as well. That thing we clambered down will be rotten in another season or two."

"Hopefully, we won't need it by then."

They journeyed in the tunnel for nearly an hour before resting. Then they continued on again. The light of their lanterns flickered.

After a while, Javan stopped. "We must be under the palace."

"Know that in your heart, do you?"

No." Lantern waving, Javan pointed to another ladder. "I know it by the way up."

As Javan climbed onto the ladder, Rogan hesitated, looking past it to the tunnel beyond.

"Huh."

Javan stopped his ascent. "What is it, sire?"

"The tunnel beyond, it looks kind of rough, half collapsed."

"As you said, it wasn't made to last forever, even with pitch and gravel."

"Perhaps we should've sought out the makers of the Lebbon circle for this project, aye? But seeing as this is a tunnel that goes against their design."

Javan didn't laugh.

"Come marvel at the length of Rogan's tunnel," the barbarian chuckled. "Long and thick but still effective, even if aged."

"Uncle, perhaps we should move in silence from here on out? We don't want to announce our presence."

"Let them come," Rogan grunted. "I prefer that to sneaking around like a rat in the sewers."

Shaking his head, Javan climbed up the rungs. Rogan followed. Metal ground on stone and dust fell onto his head. He blinked grit from his eyes, and choked down a sneeze. The hatch open, Javan slipped up and out of sight. Once Rogan had joined him, they found themselves in a storeroom full of clothing and boots. They quickly extinguished their lanterns, and placed them on the floor.

"Interesting locale for an escape hatch," Javan commented as he wrestled with a number of hanging gowns and dresses, dangling like heavy drapes through the room.

"It is a few floors down but not far from the King's chamber."

Javan tried the door to the room and found it unlocked. He eyed Rogan.

Rogan arched an eyebrow. "Trusting bastards, aren't they?"

"This is too easy," Javan said.

Short swords out, they cautiously headed into the hallway. Rogan motioned in the direction of the stairs, and they headed toward them. Ascending a floor, they looked down an empty, unlit corridor, and then went up another floor. This hall held a few dim, sputtering candles that cast eerie shadows on the walls and tapestries. Rogan pushed past Javan and crept to a large nearby door. Javan glided after him.

"King's bedchamber," Rogan whispered. "Unguarded, so we know he is not in there."

They climbed to another floor and still saw no one about.

"Awfully deserted," Javan observed.

"It is very early," Rogan replied, "but I doubt things are running like typical palace life."

At last they arrived at the floor of the great throne room, and it was here in the well-lit hallway that they saw their first signs of life. A short man of considerable age, with a tidy mustache, a thin, gray beard, and dressed in the fine clothes of the king's inner circle, rounded the corner and nearly crashed into them. He jumped back, gasping.

"Emrys," Javan hissed. "You're alive!"

"By the gods ..." Emrys kept his voice low. His eyes darted both directions in the hallway and then back to the pair. "Rogan the great ... and the general's son?"

"Javan," he named himself, frowning a little.

"Not everyone finds you memorable," Rogan told Javan. Then, glaring at Emrys, he grabbed the little man with one hand around the neck and lifted him off the floor. Emrys' feet kicked and flailed. Rogan put him down again, loosening his grip, but keeping hold of his neck. "We are here to see the king."

Coughing, Emrys stared at the pommel of the broadsword over Rogan's left shoulder and the short sword in his right hand.

"I bet you are," he rasped.

Rogan nodded down the hallway. "That is still the way to the throne room and the adjacent antechamber?"

Emrys nodded. "Of course. The current ... king ... sits there even now."

Javan nudged Rogan's sword hand. "Sire?"

"We'll get to Karac in a moment." Rogan continued to glower down at Emrys. "I'm debating what to do with him first. I suppose we should cut his throat quietly, though if anyone should find the body and raise the alarm..."

"No," Emrys pleaded, his voice still hoarse. "I can assist you, my Lord. I have no love for the usurper."

Rogan removed his hand from around the man's neck, sheathed his short sword, and fingered Emrys's garments. "And yet you wear the fineries of his court."

"Some of us fight and rebel in different ways, sire. Not all of us are skilled with a sword."

"Well, then. Come, and I shall teach you a thing or two."

Turning, Rogan started down the hall. Javan and Emrys fell in behind him.

"Why," Rogan asked, "is there no guard if the King is here?"

"The King has guards aplenty, Rogan," Emrys whispered.

Rogan's pulse quickened as they reached the throne room. Trying the door, he found it unlocked. His heart fell a little as he twisted the handle and shoved the heavy wooden door open. Within the chamber, lit by the somber moonlight filtering in through the stained-glass windows and a number of flickering candles spread about, he found no guards. Scanning the room in the weird light, Rogan spotted someone on the throne—a slumped, shrouded figure, sporting long twisted dreadlocks of hair not native to Albion.

Turning to Javan, he mouthed, *"Karac."*

They took a few steps while Emrys remained near the door. Javan went about the great table where so many war plans and domestic silliness had been debated and decided. Rogan paused for a second to gaze out an oblong window whose shutters remained open. Then he took a few more steps inside. Javan silently notched an arrow and raised his bow.

"Karac," Rogan grumbled. "Face me!"

A high-pitched peeping noise echoed in the room, drowning out his challenge. Both Rogan and Javan twitched, startled by the cry. A large bird unfurled its wings from behind the throne. Rogan thought it a parrot at first. Then it took flight, launching itself from its perch on the throne, shrieking towards Rogan. The barbarian recoiled as the dim light, revealed a reptilian body.

Javan's arrow whistled through the air, piercing the beast and knocking it to the tiled floor. It squawked twice, and then lay still. The figure on the throne didn't move or react. Javan hurried over to his uncle's side. The two looked down at the dead creature.

"Fuck me pink," Rogan muttered. "What's that?"

"Wings of a bat, body of a snake, head of an eagle?" Javan re-slung his bow. "We tread in dark waters, sire."

"Karac!" Rogan roared. "Face me, you son of a bitch!"

"Sire," Javan began, "Look at the skin tone. I don't think that is—"

Full of rage, Rogan charged across the throne room and stomped up to Karac, who apparently sat with his face buried in his hands. When Rogan grabbed a handful of dreadlocks and jerked the head up, the satiny cloak covering the king fell away. Rogan gasped.

Heavy armored footsteps echoed out in the corridor.

"Sire," Javan shouted, glancing at the doorway. When he turned back to Rogan, it was his turn to gasp.

Rogan stared into the face of his son, but the visage was that of Rohain, rather than Karac. The young, deposed King was covered in sweat, and his hair been done up in dreadlocks like Karac's. His eyes were closed and his head lolled, as if asleep.

The stomps in the hallway grew louder.

"No..." Rogan's trembling hand felt his son's neck, searching for a pulse.

"Sire," Javan yelled. "We need to brace the door! Emrys, assist me."

Rogan breathed a sigh of relief as he felt Rohain's pulse. It was weak, but consistent. He dropped his son's head and ran across the room, weapons at the ready.

"Police up your cock, Javan! We've been had."

"Very observant, sire."

Emrys scurried out of their way as they reached the heavy door.

Just before Rogan slammed it shut, he beheld the two long lines of soldiers, all from Zimbabwe, rushing for the throne room. He slammed the door and threw the bolt. It clanked into place, echoing in time with the footsteps.

Rogan turned to Javan. "Can we skate about the edges up out that window?"

Javan blinked. "I might, but you ... are too big."

Something slammed against the door, shaking the massive slab in its frame.

Rogan wheeled, thinking. "There's a murder hole up behind the throne. We'll try for that."

"Sire, what about Rohain. Is he ...?"

"He lives. And if we want to keep it that way, then we need to act. Now focus, Javan!"

The door shook again as heavy axes destroyed the latch and smashed through the wood, sending splinters to the floor of the throne room.

"Too late," Rogan muttered. "Wodan!"

He shoved Javan away from him, separating them on either side of the big table. Javan drew his short sword as the door flew open. Rogan unslung his broadsword as men spilled into the chamber wielding curved swords.

"Ho, Emrys," Rogan called, yanking his short sword from its sheath. "You'll get to use a sword after all!"

He tossed the weapon to the advisor, but the erudite man avoided the blade and kept his arms folded. The sword clattered onto the floor.

"No thank you, Rogan," Emrys quipped. "I serve another king now."

Javan jumped on the table and avoided the swinging blades, and kicked one bald man in the face, pulping the attacker's nose beneath his heel. Shrieking, the man tumbled backward, clawing at his face. Javan back-flipped, landing at another spot on the table and spinning his blade. He parried two thrusts, dodged a swing, and flayed the cheek of another attacker in half.

Rogan waded into the ebon warriors, cutting a path and separating appendages from their owners. When the force beheld the old warrior and heard his battle cry, they hesitated. That moment was all that Rogan needed. He disemboweled the nearest man, beheaded the second, lopped off the hand of the third, and then leaped into the air, joining his nephew atop the table. The grand piece of furniture, now splattered with blood, tipped and swayed, but did not fall. Rogan shoulder rolled over the edge of the banquet table and impaled a smiling attacker who, just a second before, had the aged barbarian dead to rights with a crossbow. Instead, the bolt went wide, missing its mark, and taking out another of Karac's men. Swearing and slashing, Rogan swung his broadsword again and again.

Javan flipped again, moving like lightning. He killed a warrior carrying a looted Albion broadsword with an uppercut move, thrusting his blade up through the man's jaw and out the top of his skull. With a grunt, he jerked his weapon free and turned quickly, parrying another falling blade. This one was also manufactured in Albion, and the craftsmanship was apparent—because Javan's short sword shattered as the two weapons clanged together. Shouting, Javan jumped to the tiled floor, rolled through a puddle of blood as blades struck stone all about him, and scooped up a fallen spear. He impaled the closest fighter, driving the long, feathered lance into his belly. Then he yanked on the shaft, pulling the dying man closer. His victim looked surprise as Javan stole his curved blade and pushed him away. Another warrior leaped over his fallen comrade. Javan slashed at his skull. Brains splashed onto them both as the skull cap flipped off. Javan blinked the gore from his eyes as the press of men forced him away from the table.

Amidst the bloodshed, a new arrival entered the room. He walked steadily and with great calm. This was a tall black man sporting dreadlocks.

"Karac! Finally. I was beginning to wonder if you had the sack to face me."

"Hello, father," he replied, obviously struggling with his non-native tongue.

The assembly paused, breathing hard, glancing from Karac to Rogan and then back again.

"Come on then, you bleeding cunts." Rogan spat blood and raised his gore-drenched broadsword. "Overrun me. I dare you!"

Karac snarled orders to the others in his native Zimbabwe dialect. Both Rogan and Javan understood the words.

"*Alive! Alive! Mufala, take him alive.*"

The horde charged, bellowing a war cry. Shouting, Rogan jumped headlong into the fray. He killed five of them and injured two more before being overwhelmed by the crush of bodies. Soon, his legs were grappled and Rogan went down, pinned under a press of the warriors. Somewhere, he heard Emrys laughing. Face smashed to the floor, nose bleeding, Rogan twisted his head enough to spy an open window, obscured by the slender shape of Javan. The young man had been forced to retreat into this space, warding off repeated attacks from sword and spears. He stared once at Rogan, tears welling in his eyes.

"Go," Rogan choked, barely able to breathe, his mouth filling with blood.

"Rhiannon damn them!" Javan yelled, and then swung out of the window.

His attackers gasped in surprise.

"Your nephew is a fool," Karac said. "We are fifty feet in the air."

Rogan tried to respond but could only wheeze.

"Ogan," Karac ordered. "Look out that window and see how far his guts splattered."

Rogan watched as the soldier, Ogan, obeyed the command. He moved to the windowsill and leaned out to see where Javan had landed. Seconds later, his shaved head got hacked off at the neck. Javan's blade flashed outside, as if its wielder were clinging to the castle wall. Ogan's decapitated corpse fell back into the room, shooting geysers of blood on his fellow attackers. Rogan glimpsed a man, larger and darker than the rest, glare at the body. Then the man moved toward the window.

"Mufala," Karac called. "Forget the young one! He may be wily as a snake, but he cannot go far. We have what we came for."

Mufala hesitated, shaking with rage. Then he nodded.

They chained Rogan's hands and feet, and then placed an iron collar around his neck and snapped the chains to that, twisting his arms at an uncomfortable angle. Rogan gritted his teeth but refused to voice his pain, even as they nearly wrenched his arms from their sockets. Then they wrestled him up to his feet, where he was held by four heavily-muscled warriors.

Karac put Rogan's broadsword on the table.

"That is a nice pig-sticker," he said, speaking slowly to make himself understood. "But I like mine better."

He tapped the brass ball of his long spear's bottom on the floor. It knocked hollowly.

Rogan stared at him, recoiling as he saw his own features on the savage's face. Dread filled the old man, not because he was going to die, but because he wasn't dead already.

"You have me, then," he said. "I imagine you'll torture me next. You are as unimaginative and dim-witted a king as you were when you were just a slave."

Snarling, Karac backhanded Rogan. The crack reverberated through the room. Grimacing, Rogan spat several teeth onto the floor.

"I was never a slave," Karac said. "It was but a ruse to get close to the palace with my brothers! And these are my real brothers— not the white-skinned teat-suckers that share my tainted blood. Well ... except for that one."

He gestured at Rohain, still slumped on the throne.

"Come, brother. I trust that Papa Bon Deux and Maman Ezili were successful. If so, then awaken. Your long slumber is over. Wake up, and come and greet our father."

Rohain's eyes snapped open. He rose slowly, and clambered down off the throne. He paused, holding his palms upright and staring at them in wonder, as if he had never seen his hands before. Then he crossed the room and stood at Karac's side.

"Hello, brother," Rohain said. "It is good to see you again."

"And you, as well," Karac replied. "See before you? See who I have captured?"

Rogan spat out another tooth. "Congratulations."

"He does not understand," Rohain said.

"He will." Karac looked down at Rogan. "Do you hear me, old man? You will come to understand what has happened today."

"Rohain ..." Rogan mumbled through swollen, purpling lips. "I am your father. Your king. What are you—"

"King? Nay. I refuse to call you king. Rogan the Less is more fitting, eh? You are not a king for that is what is rightfully ours!"

"You are insane," Rogan croaked.

"Am I?" Rohain grinned. "That explains a lot then. What is your excuse?"

"Excuse for what?"

"Being alive. Not that you will be for long. But I suspect you'll be dead longer than I was."

Confused, Rogan struggled to question the bizarre statement. Before he could, the brass ball on the bottom of Karac's spear shaft smashed into his head. The last thing he heard before slipping into unconsciousness was the laughter of his sons.

CHAPTER 6

THE LONG NIGHT

J avan murmured thanks to the goddess for her favors as he
crept through the shadows. He also reflected gratefully on
the times he had spent climbing the towers of various
buildings for sport when he was a child. It had saved his
life. He'd fallen a short distance after beheading Ogan, but caught
the next landing jutting from the side of the palace. In time, he
maneuvered out of sight, down the tower, clinging like a spider,
and fled the grounds via the stable-hand's exit that extended over
the moat. The small bridge, used daily to bring over sacks of grain
without troubling the main entrance ramps, proved useful and a
blessing.

Afraid and alone, Javan's first thoughts were to go back the way
Rogan and he had come, but he soon discovered that it would be
impossible to access the escape tunnel, or even hide in the slums
or behind the blacksmith's hut. Karac's men stalked the streets in a
frenzy. Instead, Javan stuck to the back alleys and hid in darkened
doorways. Luckily, the moon was barely visible, hidden behind a
thick cloud cover that left the city streets in shadow.

Eventually, he decided to hide inside the temple of his goddess,

Rhiannon. It would be deserted at this time of night, and he could rest there, and figure out what to do next. It took him an hour of stealthy movement to reach the temple. Its white tower beckoned to him, calling, promising safety and shelter. When he finally reached it, Javan choked back a sob. Kneeling, he offered a silent prayer.

He moved to the grounds west of the temple, intent on accessing a servant's door that he knew led into the tower. While trying to navigate through the hedges, he heard voices speaking. Crouching, Javan crept closer, ignoring the branches scratching his face, until he could see.

Karac's two wizards stood in a garden, illuminated by flickering torchlight. Many cloaked figures encircled them. Guards and soldiers stood at the edge of the garden. Judging by their expressions and wary stance, Javan assumed the soldiers feared the magi. Javan studied their faces more closely and recognized one of them from the earlier attack—Mufala. Javan was certain that, given how Karac had spoken to him during the assault, Mufala must be the usurper's captain of the guard. The urge to shoot an arrow through the big man's eye was strong, but Javan knew better. Doing so now would be a hollow sort of vengeance, since he'd be discovered and either captured or killed before he could fire a second arrow. He focused instead on the wizards.

Although he had seen them in visions, and heard their description from Rogan and his father, this was the first time Javan had ever encountered the two sorcerers of Damballah. The old man, slight and dressed in his dusty black short coat and a multi-colored kilt, grinned a mouth of ivory teeth as he adjusted his tall hat. This was Papa Bon Deux? He looked fat and bloated, more like a toad than a powerful wizard. But then Javan considered Akibeel. The Kennebeck shaman looked fragile, as well. He generally appeared frail and weak, as if a sudden gust of strong wind might knock him over, but despite that, he possessed great power. Perhaps the same was true of Papa Bon Deux. Maman Ezili was equally unimposing to look at—an elderly woman, hobbling on two canes and swathed in a green and orange dress that flowed behind her in the dirt. A feathered hat sat crookedly on her head.

The old man said, "It is time, Maman Ezili."

Favoring her left side, she held both canes in one hand and mixed a spoon in a large bowl set up on a tripod. Maman Ezili then looked down the line of cloaked figures, and then at the soldiers.

"Even Mufala keeps his distance and his tongue quiet," she clucked.

Papa Bon Deux nodded. "That is a blessing from Damballah in itself."

She bit her thin bottom lip. "My ears twitch, Papa. We are truly watched by some lover of the light goddess."

"What of them? The darkness will blot out the light soon enough. Proceed."

Javan's heart pounded. Resisting the urge to flee, he kept still and watched as Maman Ezili walked to the first cloaked individual. She offered the bowl to their mouth, and then repeated this with the others. Javan couldn't see what was in the bowl, but whatever the concoction, it steamed. Javan frowned, wondering what was occurring.

"I still feel eyes upon me," the witch said, trembling. "Father Damballah wouldn't endow me with such knowledge if it was not so. There is someone near."

Bon Deux looked around, studying the landscape. Javan shivered as his gaze rolled across the hedge. Then the wizard turned back to her and shrugged.

"Fear not, Maman. Wouldn't he give you clear word if a light-loving spy was in our midst, rather than just a suspicion?"

She frowned and then turned to the cloaked assembly. "Now it is time for you to go forth, my babies. Go out into the world and capture the interloper. Oh, Papa ..."

"What troubles you? There is no spy—"

"No, it's not that. My mind is heavy with the years when I bore them all, four at a time."

"I remember well." Bon Deux patted her back. "And I remember the time the grace of Damballah allowed you to carry six inside of you, instead of four. It's a shame those two extra were consumed in the womb by their brethren."

"They had to make room." She raised her head, gazing lovingly at the cloaked figures. "Go now, my children. You know what to do. Fetch the one we need and return him to us, alive."

A deep hiss escaped from their ranks. The soldiers gasped and trembled in fear, but held their positions. Turning, Maman Ezili's children dropped their cloaks. Javan squinted, doubting his eyes. At first, he thought them still wearing a canvas covering, but then they slowly unfurled and extended bat-like wings. Javan shuddered. Shrieking, the creatures leaped into the air and took flight.

Maman Ezili shed a single tear as she watched them fly away.

The swelling in Rogan's face had started to go down. He knew this because he could see again, though his vision was still blurry due to the crusted blood flaking his eyelids. Weariness weighed on him, and he closed his eyes again, letting his chin droop. This brought about a burst of pain in his collarbone. Opening his eyes, he raised his head again and let the room come into focus. Slowly, as his vision cleared, he realized he was in a dank dungeon. He knew the place well. He had sentenced men here, back when he was king.

"Repent," a voice called out, "for the end of the world is nigh!"

Rogan tried to shrug, discovered that his bonds wouldn't allow it, and instead focused on his breathing. He took in a big lungful of air, and felt no pain in his chest or ribs. That was good.

"Repent," the voice shouted again. "The end of the world is nigh!"

"So you said," Rogan muttered. He glanced around the dungeon until he found the speaker. It was another prisoner—a small, unkempt boy, just a few years younger than Javan and perhaps a few years older than Rogan's daughter, Algeniz. The youth was chained to a nearby wall. His scalp was a patchwork of bald spots where his hair had fallen out, and his face was matted with filth and drool. The rags he wore dangled from his skeletal frame. The pants were covered with piss and shit stains.

Rogan's chains rattled as he experimented with them, testing their strength. Doing so sent agony coursing through his shoulders and limbs. He might be able to bend them to his will, in time—but not yet. He was in no shape to break free of his bondage. Indeed, it was taking most of his strength just to stay awake and keep his head up. He glanced again at the boy in chains adjacent to him.

"Repent, for the end of the world is—"

"Shut your ass!"

The prisoner blinked. Then he began to giggle.

"The world will be flooded soon. The Almighty has shown me. The gates will be opened and the Great Deep will flood us all. The worms of the earth shall be loosed."

"That is all I needed," Rogan muttered. "A madman for company. Except you're not even a man. You're just a boy. Wodan curse me ..."

"I am not a madman. I am a heretic. Or at least that is what they have branded me."

"I told you to shut up."

The darkness became Rogan's abode. He had no idea if it was day or night, for it was always night in the dungeon—one long, interminable twilight. He recalled ordering the windows to be bricked up when he'd first taken the throne. At the time, he had seen fit that no man would have luxury in his prisons, since he'd decreed that justice always be swift. He'd never kept prisoners for very long, preferring them to be executed immediately after their trial. Thus, conditions in the chamber were poor. Now he felt the embrace of his own edicts ... the chafing of laws he had put into action.

He thought of Javan, and wondered about his fate. His nephew had served him well these last few years. Where was the boy now? Had he fell to his death as he leapt from the palace tower? And what of those who waited in the forests and lands surrounding Albion? What of Boone and Akibeel and Xuxan and even Zenata? Would they all die without him?

He felt a cold pinprick on his chest, just below the hollow of his throat, and realized it was the tiny glass vial containing the ashes of Queen Tancorix. Apparently, his tormenters had not seen fit to strip it from him. They'd left him with his clothes, as well, apparently preferring just to steal his weapons and gear. The necklace reminded him of his newly found daughter, Andraste. As cold as her mother, Rogan doubted she would befall the same fate at the other stragglers loyal to him.

"That little bitch will melt into the forest," he muttered. "Surrounded by her savages and Troglodytes."

"Not when the rains start," his fellow prisoner replied. "All of mankind with drown in the wrath of almighty ..."

"If your God is going to drown you, then I hope He does it soon, you little prick."

"I was told to build an—"

"Shut up! By Wodan, I'd take the torture of the rack over this."

The sound of boots thudded outside the dungeon. Gritting his teeth, Rogan struggled to hold his head high and faced the door. The lock clanged and the slab swung open. Four ebony warriors entered, clad in the vestments and light armor of Albion's elite guards. They were followed by Rohain.

"Hello, father." Rohain's voice dripped with disdain.

"Rohain. You look unwell, boy."

"I look unwell? You should see yourself, father! I doubt even the livestock would sleep with you now, beaten and bloodied as you are."

Rogan's chains rattled as he tried to shrug. "My prick is still bigger than yours."

"You taunt me with your words, father, but you are not going to win this day from me. You still do not realize who you face, do you?"

The other prisoner piped up. "You all face the end of the world, soon!"

Laughing, Rohain turned to him. "Yes! You are correct, Jasper-Thal. That is very good."

"Friend of yours?" Rogan quipped.

Rohain turned back to him. "We gave you the young heretic, Jasper-Thal, to listen to so that you wouldn't feel so alone."

"But I *am* alone. I left Albion in the hands of a man, a good man whom I trained to take my throne. A son whom I ... loved." Rogan's voice cracked. "What has happened to you, Rohain? I return now to find that a filthy bastard brat has usurped the throne from you. And you are in league with him? Whatever happened to that boy I taught to hunt and fish? What happened to the man I left in charge?"

Rohain sneered. "Can't you see it, father? Can't you see the darkness in my eyes? Surely a traveler like yourself can see that I am not who you once knew."

"Well, you're right about that. You look and smell like my son, but he had not your anger, envy or malice. I know of only one thing that can produce such a change in the soul. I am not an educated man, but I can smell deviltry like dung on a wagon. You are not my son."

"Ah, but there you are wrong." Rohain grinned. "I am not Rohain, but I am your son. We have met once before, but only briefly. Our encounter was cut short by that cowardly nephew of yours. He shot two arrows into my back. Then you cut off my arm and my head."

Rogan shook his head. "That description fits only one battle I've fought, and that only recently. How do you know of it, Rohain?"

"Because I am not Rohain. I am Karza, the bastard son you slew. I am brother to Karac, son of Destra, slave girl of Kush, who once knew you, so long ago in the royal harem of the Sultan before you came to Albion. Do you recall Destra?"

Rogan sighed. "Rohain ... son ... you know this is not true. I see now that I was wrong. It is not deviltry or sorcery that is afoot. They have done something to your mind."

"No," Rohain yelled, stalking forward until he was inches from Rogan's face. "I am Karza. I am he who you beheaded at sea!"

Rogan lunged, the chain snapping his body tight. "Then take these damned chains off and I'll do it again, you little shit!"

The soldiers raised their weapons and moved toward him. Rogan spat at them.

"You fear not a caged old man? Come closer, little pricks, and I will bite off your balls!"

The tallest of the guards reached back and swung hard, meaning to backhand the old man. Rogan drew back against the wall. The soldier was forced to reach farther to strike him. Rohain shouted a warning. As he did, Rogan jogged his position and wrapped the chains around the soldier's arm. With a boot on the foreigner's thigh, Rogan gritted his teeth and clamped down his hold with the wrapped chain. In an instant, he yanked the man's arm from its socket.

As they pulled the shrieking soldier out of the room, Rogan laughed.

"Do you recall Destra?" Rohain asked again.

"Do you recall every whore that dropped her body on yours? No, I *do not* recall her! Now stop this petty questioning. They have hypnotized you or something, Rohain. Remember who you are!"

"Did you not hear me? I am not Rohain. I am your son, Karza, whom you killed. My spirit has been pulled from the netherworld to inhabit Rohain's flesh."

Rogan struggled to keep his voice and expression calm. Inside, he seethed with rage ... and fear.

"Rohain. Karza. Whichever son of mine you are, run along and play now. Your father needs a nap. And perhaps some beer. Bring a flagon for Jasper-Thal over there, as well."

At the mention of his name, the other prisoner began to writhe in his chains. "Repent! Repent, for the end is nigh!"

"That's right," Rogan laughed. "Repent, you bastards!"

"You should be the one to repent," Rohain said. "I know what happened to Destra. I know what you did in the Sultan's bedchamber."

Rogan stared at him for a long moment. Then, he said, "What do you want? An apology? What do I care for the life of a chamber slut? If what you say is true, and you really are Karza, then go boil your balls and cut out my heart—if you have manhood left enough to do it, that is."

"You will care," Rohain promised. "Your evil has come back to haunt you."

"You are insane, boy. Your mother wasn't Destra, she was the crown queen of ..."

"I am Karza, reborn in this new flesh. By the magic of the wizard, I have returned—"

"Spare me. Your mind is fractured. It happens. You're as crazy as that fool hanging over there on the wall."

"Repent—"

"I am a barbarian," Rogan said, his head held high. "Kill me and let me bleed, for I shall not beg for my life."

"Then your life will be for naught!"

Rogan laughed. "You are telling me."

Rohain's eyes narrowed. He stared at the vial around Rogan's neck. After a moment, he reached out and snatched it away with one fist. Then he tossed it at the wall, shattering the glass. Tancorix's ashes spilled into the crevices in the floor. Wheeling around, Rohain stalked toward the door. The guards marched after him. As the latch clanked back into place, Rogan heard his son's words echo in the dungeon.

"Soon, you will see, father. Soon, we will show you the error of your ways."

Rogan let his head fall, resting his chin on his broad chest. His skin felt tight, as if he were being pricked by thousands of hot needles. When he drew breath, he thought his lungs might burst from the rage he felt inside.

"Repent," Jasper-Thal advised him quietly. "Your end is near. It comes with the dawn."

Rogan sighed. "If that is true, then morning can't get here soon enough."

CHAPTER 7

RED DAWN

Boone arose before dawn and crawled from his tent. He watched the Kennebeck braves and Xuxan's sailors interacting with each other. It bothered him that even here, on the brink of war, they did not interact with him and his men. He decided that he would speak to Xuxan and Akibeel about it after breakfast. The bonds between them needed to be strengthened. If not for war (assuming Rogan and Javan's mission was successful) then at the very least to protect them all against any Pryten treachery—or that of the Troglodytes.

Hearing the grass rustle behind him, Boone glanced in that direction and saw Akibeel emerging from the woods. The old shaman raised his hand in greeting, and carefully made his way up the hill, leaning on his cane. Boone watched his approach with some bemusement. These Kennebeck people that Rogan and Javan had brought with them were a strange bunch, and Boone was fascinated by them.

Akibeel reached him, breathing hard. "May I join you?"

"I would be honored." Boone gestured at the ground next to him.

Akibeel shook his head, declining. "No, thank you. If I sit down, then I'll just have to get back up again."

"You speak our language well. Did Javan teach you?"

"Not exactly. He helped, but my magic helped more."

Boone nodded. Talk of sorcery had always made him uncomfortable, so he decided to change the subject.

"You are up early."

Akibeel chuckled. "When you get to be my age, you'll find that your prick wakes you up at all hours. Only to make water, though. Never to fuck. Not anymore."

Boone threw his head back and laughed. Akibeel smiled, seemingly pleased by his reaction. He then stifled a yawn.

"Tired?" Boone asked.

"Very. I traveled far last night."

"You ... left the camp? I would advise against that very strongly. The Pryten wilderness is no place for—"

"I was in my tent all night," Akibeel interrupted.

"But you just said you travelled far?"

"Up here." Akibeel touched his finger to the side of his head. "My spirit can travel while my body remains where it is."

"I ... see. And where did you, um ... travel? What was your destination?"

"I went home." The old man's voice turned sad. "I missed our lands and our people, and I wanted to see them again, so I flew across the ocean and checked on things. They are doing well. Our village flourishes now that Rogan has defeated Amazarak."

"This was the wizard Javan told me about? The one who aligned himself with one of the Thirteen?"

Akibeel made some sort of strange gesture with his hand, and then nodded solemnly.

"I should like to see your land one day," Boone said.

"So would I," Akibeel replied. "In person again, rather than as a disembodied spirit."

"You miss it greatly?"

"I do. But I am indebted to Rogan and Javan, and if I must, I will die helping them see this through. They assisted me in regaining freedom for my people. I must assist them in doing the same for their kind."

"Hopefully it won't come to dying."

Akibeel shrugged. "We shall see."

They made small talk for a few more minutes, and Akibeel told Boone more about Rogan and Javan's adventures abroad. Then he excused himself and went off to find breakfast. Boone sat for a while longer, enjoying the solitude. The sounds from camp melded into background noise, along with the birds. Feeling at peace, he watched the sun rise. When it had crested the horizon, Boone climbed to his feet. He smelled the smoke from the cook fires. His stomach grumbled. Sighing, he glanced toward the border of Albion.

"You're thinking of Rogan."

"Hello, Andraste." Boone grimaced. "I didn't hear you approach. You should be more cautious coming up behind me. I could have mistaken you for an enemy."

"You may, still."

"If that was your attempt at flattery, you must do better. And yes, to answer your question, I am thinking about Rogan—and my half-brother, Javan."

"Do you think they will never return?"

Boone shrugged. "That would be my guess. Damn foolish mission, if you ask me."

"And you are stuck with Rogan's bitch daughter, at the mercy of her whims and savage forces"

"You can only kill me once, beast girl. If you're going to, then have mercy and do it now. I'd prefer that rather than your attempts to bore me to death with conversation."

Andraste didn't respond. Her attention was on the sky. Frowning, Boone slowly followed her gaze.

"Big buzzards out this way, huh?"

"Those aren't buzzards." Andraste turned to him, her eyes wide with alarm. "Ready your men!"

She shouted out orders in the Pryten tongue. Her people responded immediately, bringing their axes and arrows to bear as the rest of the army stared at them in confusion. Boone stared at Andraste, not understanding what was happening, and then turned back to the flying figures again. His eyes widened. Now that they were closer, he understood her panic. What he'd mistaken for a flock of carrion birds were, in reality, a group of flying men with long wings jutting from their backs.

Boone shouted to his men to take up arms. He saw Akibeel and Xuxan do the same with their respective people. The Kennebeck natives notched arrows and raised their bows while the sailors from Olmek-Tikal drew their swords and cutlasses. Boone's troops quickly spread out into formation. The only group missing was the Troglodytes. His back to the approaching enemy, Boone was so engrossed in surveying the defense preparations, that he didn't see Akibeel gesturing wildly and shouting at him until it was almost too late.

"Duck," the old shaman yelled. "Behind you!"

Hearing the snap of wings behind him, Boone flung himself face forward into the grass. His chainmail scraped his ribs as he went down. He rolled, seeing the monster men flying directly overhead. Wheeling, one of them dove toward him. As he struggled to rise and draw his sword, Boone heard Akibeel give the order to fire. The Kennebeck loosed a volley at their attackers. The arrows zinged through the air, followed a second later by those of the Prytens. A cry of dismay went up from both the archers and Boone as they watched the missiles bounce off the flock's hides.

The creature swooping down on Boone clawed at him with its long legs. He sidestepped, narrowly missing the beast's black talons, and swiped at its calves with his sword. The blade reverberated as if he'd struck a tree. Screeching, the winged man-thing rose into the air, circling around for another strike.

"Damn things have a hide like a crocodile," Boone gasped. "Pike-men! Come up!"

On his knee, sword out, Boone desperately looked for the

squad. The stout group charged toward him, all carrying heavy pointed pikes with shafts thicker than a weaver's beam. Their stature was such that their heavy centers of gravity were the key to such a force, deployed at certain stages of a war to form a line that would stop any advancing army. Though not usually an attack force, the pike-men nevertheless stood their ground and readied for the winged beasts to get after them. Boone saw the fear on their faces, but felt an immense burst of pride that they followed his order without question.

The winged men circled and swooped, pestering the troops but not butchering anyone.

"They're not trying to slaughter us," Boone said aloud. "They're just causing mayhem."

One of the pike-men threw up a lucky strike and nailed a beast in the groin. The heavy point of his weapon stuck and he pulled the thing down to the ground. The frenzied creature flopped about, shrieking as the pike-man's brethren pierced the beast a dozen times.

"There aren't but a few dozen of them!" Seeing that his forces greatly outnumbered these things, Boone looked toward the open country. "I see no other army ..."

Shoving him aside, Andraste took out what—at first glance—appeared to be a spreading fan, but was in fact a spread of small throwing knives. She began heaving them at the passing creatures, but the blades had no effect.

"They are after something," she cried.

"Yes," Boone shouted. "Our lives!"

She shook her head and started to reply, but before she could, one of the monsters fell to the ground between them, dead. An arrow jutted from its eye. Another creature screeched above them, enraged. Before Boone or Andraste could react, two more arrows plunged into each of its eyes. It plummeted down to the earth, crashing onto its kin. The two of them turned to see Zenata notching two more arrows. She winked at Boone, then glared at

Andraste and spat at her feet. Then she darted off into the fray, firing her bow again.

"Bitch," Andraste snarled.

"And she has reason to be, at least where you are concerned. And yet, despite that, she still just saved your life. Perhaps you should be more grateful."

"I'll show her my gratitude by giving her to a Troglodyte to mate with."

They spun at the sound of Akibeel screaming, his cries shrill enough to be heard over the cacophony of battle. The old shaman kicked and fought as he was lifted off the ground by two of the creatures, who had seized his arms with their clawed feet. As soon as they had him aloft, they headed toward the edge of the trees, and then veered toward the border.

"Hold your fire," Boone ordered. "You'll hit the old man!"

As Akibeel's captors spirited him away, the other creatures climbed higher into the air and departed as well. The ragtag army could do nothing but watch in despair and disbelief as they disappeared into the sunrise with the old man as their prisoner. Zenata charged after them, running across the grassland, but she was no match for their speed.

"Zenata," Boone called. "Come back! You'll never catch them."

Ignoring him, she raced over the hill and vanished.

"Let her go," Andraste said. "Why would they take the old man?"

Boone shook his head. "I do not know."

The Kennebecks fell to the ground and wailed at the loss of their shaman, beating their chests and pulling their own hair out by the roots. Xuxan watched, shaking his head sadly.

"Damn it!" Boone stabbed the ground with his sword. "We sit here, waiting. And this is what happens. We should have marched on the city instead."

"You will get no argument from me," Andraste agreed.

"Sir!" One of the soldiers waved at him to join them.

Boone stomped over, followed by Andraste, and then Xuxan.

They surrounded the body of the monster the pike-man had killed. Black blood oozed from its wound. Up close, the thing appeared more reptilian than human. It had fangs, pits for a nose, and snake-like eyes. Worse, it seemed to be undergoing some supernatural metamorphosis—a biological devolution. As they watched, its scales fell off like a wilting plant losing its petals. The stench that wafted up from it was horrendous. Then the beast began to shrink in size. Within a minute, the body of a human infant lay amidst the shed scales and blood. A quick glance confirmed that the same thing occurred with the two creatures that Zenata had killed.

"This is what we face?" Xuxan's expression was horrified. "How can we fight such things?"

Boone glared at him. "You say Rogan led you in the other world across the sea?"

"I wasn't there for it. He sailed with my friend, Captain Huxria. But I adventured with Rogan before that, and I am told that while he was with Akibeel's people, he fought monsters and a devil named Meeble."

"Do not speak of the Thirteen," Boone cautioned.

"I beg your pardon," Xuxan apologized, "but I must speak of another member of that group."

"Why?"

"Because with my own eyes I have seen Rogan fight one of the spawn of Dagon on our journey here."

Boone clapped him on the back. "And if Rogan can do that, Xuxan, can you not live by his example and do the same?"

"I am not Rogan. I am just Xuxan. And I am a long way from home."

"Rogan always finds a way," Boone assured him. "He always finds a way. And so must we."

Andraste giggled. "Hope in one hand and shit in the other, see which fills up the fastest."

Smiling, Boone turned to her and said sweetly, "Then give me your hand, fair maiden."

CHAPTER 8
KINGDOM OF THE BASTARDS

Rogan judged that it was a few hours into morning when they came for him again. The sunlight that spilled into the dungeon when the door was flung open confirmed his suspicions.

Six guards filed into the room, heavily armored and weapons held at the ready. He saw the silhouettes of more standing out in the hall. Then another soldier entered the room, taller than the others. Rogan recognized him as Mufala.

"Took you long enough," Rogan grumbled. "I thought perhaps you intended to kill me with boredom, rather than the implements of execution."

Instead of responding, Mufala took a whip of many tails from his belt and uncoiled it.

"Remember," he told the other soldiers in his native dialect, "even in chains, he is still dangerous."

Rogan was about to respond using the language of Zimbabwe, but Mufala turned and lashed out with the whip. It cracked through the air, encircling his arms. Before Rogan could react, Mufala had ensnared his forearms and drawn them tight into a noose. Only then did he approach the prisoner.

"What do you think of this, Jasper?" Rogan called to his fellow prisoner.

"I feel pity for you," Jasper replied, "but take heart in the fact that all of them will soon drown in the great flood that is to come!"

Rogan grinned. "It cannot come soon enough."

They unchained Rogan from the wall and dragged him out of the cell. His hands were bound with a long chain that connected to a ring around his throat, and to a second and third ring around each of his ankles. His feet had chains between them, as well. Rogan could shuffle, but it took all of his concentration just to keep his balance. It was only after they had him in the corridor that Mufala removed the whip. Rogan gritted his teeth to keep from wincing. He was glad to have the use of his legs back again, but they ached and tingled from his time in the cell.

They pulled and prodded him through a twisting network of corridors and stone staircases. Rogan noted that none of the old guards from his time were present—only the black men who had come here with Karac. He tested his bonds once, but his arms were numb, and the action aroused Mufala's attention, earning Rogan a poke in the back with the tip of a pike. After that, he marched along in acquiescence.

Once out into the courtyard and the morning air, Rogan's heart was momentarily elated when he spotted the Thulite bodyguard, Donas, a hulking blonde he had made his personal friend years ago on a hunt. Rogan's excitement fell when he saw Donas open the door to the imperial chamber and bow his head. Then he hurried over to Mufala and the others. Rogan tried to meet his eye, but Donas looked away.

"Coward," Rogan muttered, earning himself another jab in the shoulder blades.

Rohain, Karac, and a dozen guards stepped through the door and into the courtyard.

"On your knees before the king!"

Donas pushed Rogan to the dirt, tearing the deposed King's pants. Rogan glared back at the Thulite, and then at his son. His eyes were drawn to the thin, jeweled iron crown on Rohain's head —a crown once placed on his own head by Thyssen. Now it was affixed around the bulky dreadlocks Rohain had apparently come to favor.

"Look at the two of you together," Rogan said, voice heavy with sarcasm. "Is this what they call brotherly love?"

Rohain and Karac smiled at one another. The guards snickered.

"It is only fitting," Karac said, "given that we are indeed brothers."

"Same father, maybe," Rogan admitted, "but very different mothers."

"No," Rohain said. "The same mother, too."

Mufala's deep voice resounded from behind Rogan. "He still has not fully contemplated what has happened. He does not understand that Karac rules alongside Karza, who now inhabits the flesh of Rohain."

"You are all mad," Rogan raged. "If you are no longer Rohain, then what claim do you have to the throne more than the usurper standing next to you?"

Karac stepped closer. "Rohain had no claim to the crown. I, Karac, am the firstborn son of Rogan, barbarian warrior. My brother Karza was the second."

"What of it? Any child from a concubine is not a recognized heir. Do you know how much seed I spread across this world? Too much to recall every slice I dropped it in, why only the other day I found out—"

"What you say is true," Karac interrupted. "And even if it were not, the people of Albion would never completely accept the rule of a black man like myself who is not of their blood. There would always be dissent. So, we have placed Karza's soul in the body of someone whose rule they will accept. Now, he sits on the throne, wearing the body of Rohain, while I stand at his side. We rule together."

Rogan's shoulders sagged as he fought to retain his composure. He looked around the courtyard as more people began to file in.

Mostly, it was populated by the black warriors wearing Albion military clothing. A few of Rogan's young advisors and politicians, who clearly still remained loyal to Rohain, stood in the background. Like Donas, they refused to meet his gaze.

"You support this madman?" Rogan yelled at his former court. "Bah! Of course, you do. You are politicians and thus, only look for bread and butter."

More figures entered the courtyard. Rogan growled when he saw the betrayer, Emrys, who had led him and Javan into a trap just the night before. Now, he led Rogan's two daughters, Erin and Algeniz. They looked at their father and the assembly in confusion. Stunned at how much they'd grown, Rogan tried to remain focused on the matter at hand.

"My father," Rohain exclaimed, addressing the crowd, "is on trial for murder. My half-brother Karac has made me aware of how Rogan, our former king, murdered not only Karac's brother, Karza, but their mother, as well."

The crowd gasped and murmured among themselves. Karac's soldiers cursed the prisoner. Mufala sneered. Emrys kept his expression calm, betraying no emotion. Erin and her little sister's confusion visibly deepened.

Rogan laughed. "You are ignorant if you seek to try me on—or inflict guilt on me—for what I have done in the past. And now you pretend to be yourself, rather than making believe you are that cursed Karza?"

"I don't know what you're talking about," Rohain said, feigning ignorance. Then he bent over to face Rogan, and winked.

Behind him, Rogan heard Mufala chuckle.

"This old man is obviously senile," Karac said to the assembly. "He seems to believe that Papa Bon Deux, great wizard of Damballah, has endowed you with the soul of Karza, my brother whom he killed."

The noise from the crowd grew louder.

"I'd kill him again if I could," Rogan said. "I wish that he'd had more heads I could lop off."

"And do you wish to kill his mother again?" Rohain asked. "Go on, tell them all, tell your daughters how you cut her open and let her third baby die as it fell from her womb. Tell them all!"

Erin stepped forward. "This is madness, Rohain. That is simply an embellished version of a tale from our father's own youth. Legend is that he was cut from his mother by his father."

"That is true," Rogan confirmed. "My father took me from that bitch so he could raise me a warrior."

Karac shook his head. "And you do not deny murdering my mother, Destra, or her baby, or my brother?"

Rogan shrugged as much as the chains would let him. "I've admitted I killed Karza, though when no one is listening, you two claim that he now inhabits Rohain's form. As for Destra, perhaps the third son she bore wasn't mine. Perhaps I wasn't willing to be further blackmailed by the daughter of Zimbabwe's wizards. Bah. But I never killed the infant. He could've lived, had the gods saw the means. They did not."

Many in the court gasped.

"He is mad," Karac proclaimed. "I know he is your father, Rohain, but perhaps it would be a mercy to have him put to death."

"Yes," Rogan agreed. "You should order that as king. If you've got the guts to order your father put to death. You think that you can rule this land so easily? Do you think that all will fall in line like these vermin of the court?"

Grinning, Rohain bent down and whispered. "You may be surprised. The wizard of Damballah has told a fascinating tale of a mighty war on the sea and blood in the water ... the blood of reavers drank by sharks and absorbed by the dark lord, Damballah, in sacrificial glee. There is nothing to stop me from my desire! My warriors have assassinated any general worth his oats to oppose us or any good advisor slobbering on your former glory. They were the first to fall. These weaklings around us today want only peace and comfort. Their new leader is the same as the old, only with grander ambitions for future invasions and dark destruction."

Rogan coughed, shifting his sore knees. "I had Imperial ambitions too ... when I was younger."

"Such is the nature in our savage blood, to conquer, to fight, to control and to seek adventure. That is why you are predictable, even unto death. I knew your wanderlust would come again. Papa Bon Deux's men infiltrated the slave class and soon learned of the discontent of the labor classes here in fair Albion. The taskmasters under the rule of your aged policies were ripe for change. The taskmasters make the common folk work for Albion. They followed me easily."

Rogan groaned, knowing this was a fear he had oft held. "I never trusted them or the teamsters. He wanted to replace them with loyal men from Thule."

"Perhaps you should have. Your pact with the old tribal king up north gave you warriors when you needed them, but they can't help you now. The old Thunder Wolf of Thule was nothing but a castrated mongrel. They are indeed a good backup plan for the Prytens in the wilderness, but all of that good will to the north will be for naught soon."

"Maybe you really are Karza," Rogan admitted, "because Rohain certainly never had shit for brains. The Wolf will not accept you. He hates everyone, truly the wizards who slew his daughter."

"Perhaps," Rohain admitted, "but he wouldn't get his ass out of his cave at his age."

"Try him and see. And he is not the only one. There are plenty who will oppose you."

"Oh, that reminds me, dear father. Where is Javan?"

"Go to hell."

"Hah! Papa Bon Deux assures me I will rule *there* as well if I play my cards right to Damballah! But I ask you again, where is Javan? You wouldn't want what happened to Teran to happen to him."

"What say you?"

"Teran is dead," Rohain whispered. "His head occupies a bedpost in Karac's chamber."

Rogan lunged, but his chains restrained him. Choking, he gasped for air. Mufala's whip snapped through the air and landed across his broad back. Rogan yelled, more from anger than pain. The assembly gasped. Rohain stepped back, and shook his head sadly, playing to the crowd.

"It is a shame about your son," he said loud enough for everyone to hear him. "My younger brother, Teran, killed in that terrible hunting accident. I do hope no further deaths haunt the rest of my family, father."

"If Teran is dead, then you lie about the circumstances. He would have died fighting, just like Javan."

"And again, where is Javan? We did not find him at the bottom of the tower. Therefore, he must have escaped. Where would he go? You must have some idea."

"You will get nothing from me, you bastard."

"We already have something from you," Karac gloated. "We have your daughters."

Erin and Algeniz glanced at each other, clearly troubled.

"Rohain, what does he mean?"

Smiling, Rohain waved off her concerns. "Nothing, sister. And when we are assembled like this, you really should address me as your king."

Rogan spit in the dirt. "Some king. You have no army to command. I'm told they all deserted."

"Some did," Rohain replied. "But I have my loyalists from Zimbabwe, and even now, a million other warriors from that dark country march across the expanse between our lands. We will deal with the deserters soon enough. First, however, we have other things to attend to."

"Will one of those things be breakfast?" Rogan taunted.

"We have a morning sacrifice for you to observe, father. Such is the way of Damballah, and that is the god that Albion now serves.

The days of the goddess are numbered. Soon, we will turn her temple into a place for the new god."

"You should turn it into a brothel instead."

"Bring him," Rohain said to the guards. "Mufala, fetch the wizards. Oh, and fetch your keepsake from your chambers. Perhaps Rogan would like to see it."

"Understood, my lord."

"Rohain," Erin demanded, "what is happening? Perhaps that tall man understands, but I do not."

"You will, soon enough."

As Mufala departed, the other guards dragged Rogan across the courtyard and placed him in a wooden wagon. Rohain rode in a chariot pulled by two great white horses. They traveled from the inner courts and through the rings of walls protecting the fair city. Rogan rested on the straw and filth in the cart. It felt like a fine bed after his night in the dungeon. The streets were empty, but still neat. Rogan wondered if all the populace hid inside, awaiting judgment or word of what was to come. He remembered how equally empty they had been when he and Javan had snuck inside. Surely, they had not all fled?

Rogan thought of Erin and Algeniz. What was in store for them? Poor Algeniz, a lovely child and the glowing reminder of her mother, the queen, who had died giving birth to her. He thought of Teran, his chest filled with fear that perhaps Rohain spoke the truth about the boy. And if so, what other truths was Rohain telling? Could the young king really be Karza reincarnated? Was Rohain's spirit really gone, never to return? He thought of Boone and Andraste and Akibeel and the young warrior girl, Zenata.

And then, he thought of Javan, and wondered himself what had happened to the boy.

Soon, far outside of the city, they reached the edge of the Severin river. Rogan swallowed hard as he saw the supplication point of unknown gods.

JAVAN WATCHED AS ROHAIN'S PROCESSION RODE AWAY. FROM HIS perspective, high in the tower of the deserted temple of Rhiannon, Javan had a great view of the city. He could see the stadium nearby and wished he could compete there again soon. However, considering recent events, he doubted if things would ever be the same in fair Albion again. He wondered again what had happened to all the priests and acolytes who had served and lived here. Had they fled, deserting the city and their goddess? Were they in chains, somewhere in the castle dungeon? Or hiding in the city? Or dead?

He was just about to descend from the tower and attempt to follow Rogan, when he spotted a group of fifteen soldiers marching toward the temple. Even from this height, he could hear their booted feet on the cobblestones. Soon, they smashed down the ornate wooden doors and entered the inner sanctum. Javan scrambled down into the attic crawlspace and peered through a small knothole in the floor, watching as the soldiers removed the wooden altars and tiny stone slabs put in places ages ago. Laborers arrived, and set about their tasks—emptying the temple of all of its furnishings. They worked throughout the day, and Javan cursed the delay. By now, he'd have no way of tracking Rogan. Instead, he could do nothing but watch helplessly as they further defiled Rhiannon's temple by replacing the altars with tiny ivory benches worthy of their heathen gods. These works, crafted from the tusks and bones of elephants, were well made but screamed heresy to Javan.

Around noon, the shriveled sorceress Maman Ezili arrived, now dressed in a red skirt, green tunic, and fluttering, wide-stitched purple robe. Javan watched in revulsion as she danced in the belly of the temple, rocking back and forth on her crutches. Then she chanted and slaughtered a few chickens. Quickly, she spread their blood in a five-pointed star design on the temple floor. Over and over again, she reinforced this design with more blood. When she was finished, she motioned at the door.

Javan nearly cried out. His young heart raced as two warriors entered with a small figure in their grasp. It was Akibeel! The old shaman was brought into the temple sanctum and stripped nude. When he saw the design on the floor, Akibeel tried to resist, earning himself a series of vicious punches and kicks. He collapsed, beaten and groaning, and they dragged him to the center of the sigil. As he lay there, the old woman giggled, licking chicken blood from her fingers. Finally, Akibeel raised his head.

"I know you," she said. "I have seen you in my dreams."

"And I have seen you in my nightmares," Akibeel responded. "Though you are far more repulsive in real life."

He stared down at the blood on the floor, tracing the lines with his gaze.

"Do you know what that is?" Maman Ezili asked. "Go ahead. Try to use your powers. They will not work."

Ignoring her, Akibeel closed his eyes.

"See?" The old woman cackled. "Where are your gods of light now? Rhiannon stays away when the dark embrace of Damballah covers her temple."

Still silent, Akibeel opened his eyes and looked up. Javan drew back from his place high on the floor, gripping the handle of his sword. He wondered if the shaman saw him. He crept over to an open air shaft, wondering if there were some way to save Akibeel. Above him were two open skylights. Below him was a great fall, with nothing to cling to. Feeling helpless, he turned his attention back to the scene below, as the soldiers left the temple. The sorceress and shaman were alone.

"Nothing to say?"

Shrugging, Akibeel changed position and sat cross-legged amidst the blood.

Maman Ezili turned as Karac's other wizard entered. "Perhaps Papa Bon Deux will loosen your tongue."

The old warlock grinned. "I see Maman Ezili has made the cage well."

Finally, Akibeel spoke. "You think that this trap of evil can keep the gods from me?"

Papa Bon Deux chuckled and ran a bony hand over his bald

head. "The cage is not to keep you or your magic in. It is to keep something else from getting out. Rhiannon will never return to a temple so defiled."

Akibeel shook his head. "Rhiannon is not my god."

"It does not matter who you worship. You are merely part of the sacrifice. We required a strong magus. Other than ourselves, you are the strongest in the region."

From above them through the sky lights came the sound of rushing air. Javan flattened against the wall and an ebony creature passed him by. He glimpsed leathery, bat-like wings, similar to those of the flying men he'd seen leave the night before, but these were much larger. If it noticed him, the thing gave no indication. Instead, it swooped down and hovered over Akibeel. What stunned Javan the most was that none of the three humans below seemed scared. Akibeel sat serene and confident, and Karac's two sidekicks seemed gleeful. Now he could see it better. It had no hair, only crocodile-like scales, and a rat-like tail curled and whipped beneath it. The beast extended a clawed foot to Papa Bon Deux. Clutched between the talons was a metal tube. The wizard accepted the gift, opened the tube, and produced a scroll from inside.

"Thank you, my Lord Damballah," Papa Bon Deux exclaimed.

Javan trembled with fear at the mention of the name.

Flapping its mighty wings, the demon of the netherworld arose toward the shaft. Javan hid again as it soared past him and vanished out the skylights. Javan looked down and saw Papa Bon Deux unrolling the scroll.

"I am rewarded for my labors!" Bon Deux held up the scroll and a tiny object that had been wrapped in it.

"That scroll's flesh tone is lighter, like from the Eastern lands," Maman Ezili replied. "That must be ancient indeed."

She took the small object from her compatriot and put it on the end of a long wooden lance. As Papa Bon Deux started to read from the scroll of human flesh, Maman Ezili moved to the edge of the sigil and shoved the lance at Akibeel.

"Open your mouth! Take the gift of Damballah and see if this Rhiannon protects you."

"I told you, Rhiannon isn't my god, and my gods cannot reach me in this place."

Moving into position, Javan reached for his bow and notched an arrow.

Papa Bon Deux's voice grew louder. Javan didn't recognize the language he was reciting. Maman Ezili jabbed at Akibeel's face with the lance, but missed. Javan drew back on his bowstring and took aim.

"No," Akibeel cried out. "This is the end. I am helpless here, far from my home."

His gaze was fixed high on Javan's hiding spot, but the sorcerers seemed to think he was speaking to them. Javan knew what he was doing. He feared that if Javan shot one of the wizards, he would give away his hiding place. But if he didn't, their plans for the old shaman—whatever they might be—would come to fruition. Javan's arms trembled. His arrow shook. Sweat poured into his eyes.

"I am resigned to my fate," Akibeel shouted.

"That's right," the witch said. "You are. Now take Damballah's gift. Eat of it."

"I will not." Closing his eyes again, Akibeel began to chant in the Kennebeck tongue.

Sighing, she stabbed him in the throat with the tip of the lance. Javan tried not to scream. His arrow slipped from his bow and clattered onto the floor. Papa Bon Deux finished the incantation. For a second, Javan feared the man had heard his arrow fall, but then he realized that the wizard was moving to stand beside the witch. The two of them watched Akibeel, choking and bleeding out in the middle of the sigil.

"The offering went in through the wound," Maman Ezili reported.

"Good," Bon Deux said. "Once it is born, it shall crave more blood. To keep it caged here, we will need to provide more, every so often."

Akibeel fell on all fours, his mouth working soundlessly. His hands went from the wound in his throat to his abdomen. Suddenly, he flopped onto his belly in the center of the bloody star. The back of his breeches fluttered, and a tiny, bloody creature crawled out of Akibeel's hind quarters.

Javan holstered his bow and hugged the wall, praying to Rhiannon. When she didn't answer, he prayed to every other god he could think of, including Rogan's. He closed his eyes, but opened them again when he heard a tapping sound below, punctuated by a wet sucking noise.

Looking over the edge, Javan saw the tiny creature running around the sigil, trying to find a way to go past its boundaries. It made a noise like that of a baby goat.

The body of Akibeel was no more.

Javan's body shook as he wept in silence, muffling his sobs with his arm so that the wizards wouldn't hear him.

CHAPTER 9
UNEXPECTED ALLIES

Because his father was a general, Boone had always insisted on doing the same duties as the rest of his troops. He never wanted to be accused of favoritism or nepotism, or have his valor or bravery challenged. He was first into battle, and first to dig a latrine, if a hand was needed in doing so. That's why he was on watch, perched atop a hill, when he saw someone approaching the camp.

"You are up early again," Andraste said, sneaking up behind him.

Boone grunted, eyes affixed on the onrushing figure. It wasn't until she drew closer that he recognized the one breasted girl from the far off land. She ran like mad toward the camp, waving her arms and shouting in her native language.

"Zenata," Andraste said. Her tone was one of distaste.

The young warrior continued to yell in her language. When Boone frowned, she slid to a halt in front of him and changed to his tongue.

"An army is on the way here! Huge!" She bent, hands to her dirty legs, trying to breathe. "Thousands of them, right behind me."

Boone's frown deepened. "Where?"

Still breathless, Zenata pointed. Boone jumped on his horse, pausing only to glare at Andraste who leapt on her mount, bareback, and followed along. Once at the crest of the valley between them and the next tree line, they saw the enormous mass of humanity and horses moving in from the north. Using a scope, he watched the forces and smiled.

"I'll alert our forces," Andraste said, panicked.

"No need."

Noting his smile, Andraste snapped, "Care to share in the joke?"

"They are ours, in theory. They fly the banner of the Albion military, but there is a red slash across each one."

"What does that mean?"

Boone pulled open his chainmail armor and bent down so that she could see the area of his skin over his heart. An identical red slash had been tattooed on the spot. "It is the sign of Thyssen, my father, of our household."

"Your father ..."

"Come, let us wake the camp and prepare a welcome." He looked back and grinned wide. "General Thyssen approaches."

They galloped back to the encampment and roused their forces. Then Boone, Andraste, and Xuxan rode back out to the hillside to await the army. Zenata ran along behind them, having recovered from her cross-country dash. Boone's forces wandered up the hillside as well, eager to see their countrymen. They were followed by curious Kennebeck, the sailors from Olmek-Tikal, and a number of Prytens who did not trust the new arrivals and were wary for their queen.

"Javan bears no such mark on him," Andraste said as they watched Thyssen's regiment draw closer. "I've seen him naked."

At her words, Zenata snarled, lips peeled back from her teeth.

Boone quickly said, "Javan is young and not a full soldier."

"Spare me your rituals." Andraste waved him off. "That's quite a force he's coming up with."

Bonne nodded. "Father would go to war naked, but in regular times, he is quite shrewd."

She sighed. "Better have someone ride out to explain my folk are all on the same side as him now. Those long bowmen are already notching arrows."

The army had everything needed for an invasion or siege. In addition to the long bowmen, there were companies of men with smaller bows and crossbows, groups of pike-men carrying stiff poles, lance hurlers who would fight with short swords after throwing their light projectiles, stealthy bolo slingers, companies of spearmen, several groups of both light and armored cavalry, and in the far rear horse-drawn wagons with small siege devices for long distance firing.

As the group in front of the army parted their horses, up rode the general himself, flanked by a burly adjutant on each side. Thyssen stood six and a half feet tall and sat upon a draft horse, fitting for his thick, tree-trunk frame. He wore light armor and his helmet hung from one of his saddle bags. A long sword sheathed on his mount, Thyssen also sported daggers on his belt and a shorter blade as well. His long white hair had been tied behind his back, but his bushy beard hung to his chest. Even at such an early hour, his face, burnt red by the sun and weathered by years of exposure, was covered in sweat. His eyes were alert, and his countenance grim.

"Boone," Thyssen grunted. He glanced at the Pryten queen and then back to his son. "Good to see you."

"General," Boone saluted, as did the others of the Albion stripe.

Thyssen waved lightly and cleared his throat. "Nice territory. Damn, I gotta piss."

He swung his leg down and stood by his horse and did just that.

Andraste looked at Boone. "And you call us barbarians."

"I'm right fuckin' here, sugar dumplings," Thyssen grumbled, shaking his member. "Maybe you'd like to assist?"

Andraste raged. "I'll cut that old prick right off you and ..."

"You'll shut yer ass is what you'll do, honeysuckle. If I fart in the wrong direction, you'll be so full of arrows they'll make a quiver of yer twat." He then put his cock away and exhaled. "Now then, Boone, what company are ya keepin' these days?"

Boone explained their situation, and Thyssen smiled at the news of Rogan and Javan's return. He eyed the foreign warriors with interest. Boone warned about the Troglodytes lurking in the forest just beyond the camp, but Thyssen showed no fear or surprise. Then Boone mentioned Javan's sacrifice for the good of the army. The general looked at Zenata and smirked.

"What?" Zenata asked.

Thyssen gave an amiable shrug. "Came a long way in the world to just get yer heart ripped out, huh, kid? Well, get used to it. Life sucks ass, considerably more the older one gets. It's amazing what ya gotta do in life to win a war or crush your foes, but you'll do it."

"Careful, old man." Andraste held up a throwing axe. "You can still go to war with no balls."

"Honey child, we both know that ain't true."

Suddenly, Andraste stumbled backward. She looked at her hand, eyes wide. A bolo was wrapped around her wrist and the tomahawk. Before she could react, a second bolo whipped through the air and wrapped around her throat. Gagging, she staggered further, out of range of the general.

Thyssen stuffed his penis away and stomped toward her, seizing a handful of her hair. The Pryten warriors drew arms, but Andraste held up a hand to stop them. She glared at Thyssen, choking.

"Go ahead," he snarled. "Tell your people to attack. We'll cut them down before they reach ya. Call on your ghoulies in the forest. Yer pissin' up the wrong rope, deary dear."

"Father," Boone said, "perhaps you—"

Interrupting with a wave of his hand, Thyssen released Andraste and motioned to one of his adjutants. "Cut her loose. If she talks again, cut out her tongue. Archers, if her people so much as move, drop them where they stand."

As the adjunct stepped forward, Thyssen turned to Boone, regarding him lightly.

"It is good to see ya, son. And I am glad at the news of yer brother and Rogan."

"It is good to see you, as well, father."

Andraste clutched her throat, gasping for air. When she removed her hand, Boone spotted a bright red welt completely encircling her neck.

"Pryten Queen," Thyssen said, "if you've still got a voice left, translate to yer people. Boone, do Rogan's foreigners understand our tongue?"

"Some do. Captain Xuxan and Zenata can translate for those who do not."

Nodding, Thyssen turned to the assembled throng. His voice boomed. "We all will fight together for this campaign and prolly all go back to hating each other when it's over, but for now, we need to be as one. Got me?"

He paused, allowing his words to be translated. Many of the Prytens grumbled among themselves.

"If you don't want to fight alongside us," Thyssen continued, "then ya can be babies and go back in the woods, back to wiping yer asses on leaves, but know this—these fuckers from the south, these soldiers of Karac, will come to kill and screw you all next once I'm dead. Either stand with me or be thrown onto the pile of those corn holed into slavery by these bastards. Ya got me?"

This time, the Prytens shrugged or grunted in agreement.

"I've lived a long time to die in such a way, so pardon the fuck outta me if I'm not worried about kindness to a bastard girl, her army of sheep fuckers and a bunch of ghouls that are so goddamned ugly they have to hide in the forest. I'm gonna face my god today or tomorrow, so what the fuck is all this to that?"

This elicited cheers from the Albion soldiers. The Prytens glowered, but the foreigners laughed. Thyssen addressed them next.

"And as for you red and brown folk, who I'm told came here

with my old friend Rogan. You fought for him. Will ye fight for me? Because as soon as Karac is done with this lot, he'll be crossing the ocean and coming for you."

After Xuxan and Zenata had translated, the sailors and Kennebeck warriors voiced their solidarity.

"Now then," Thyssen sighed. "Got any wine? Mine's 'bout out."

———

JAVAN STRETCHED CAREFULLY, TRYING TO EASE THE KINKS IN HIS neck, back and legs without alerting the wizards to his presence. He despaired how the Temple of Rhiannon—a place he'd come for refuge—had now instead become his prison. He was desperate to leave and find Rogan before whatever Karac had in store befell him, but he couldn't escape as long as the wizards remained below. All he could do was watch and wait and try not to tremble with fear or despair.

Peering over the side at the bloody pentagram again, Javan beheld an ethereal emerald glow in one of the points, but couldn't see the tiny beast Papa Bon Deux had conjured. He knew it lurked there. He could hear the tiny taps of its hooves, punctuating the chuckling of Papa Bon Deux, and the screechy tones of Maman Ezili. Javan's stomach groaned, aching for sustenance. He massaged his belly, trying to suppress the urge.

Suddenly, the torches flickered as the temple door swung open. A black man entered. Javan recognized him from the ambush in the castle. Karac had called this man Mufala. He glanced at the wizards, and then at the tiny beast prancing about inside the constraints of the sigil.

"Dare not smudge the blood-line, Mufala," Papa Bon Deux warned. "Our pet must remain caged!"

"I have been sent to fetch you," Mufala replied. "Karac and Karza say it is time. We are to meet them along the banks of the river."

"And Rogan's daughters?"

"They are with him. Everything is ready."

"Then let us be off," Papa Bon Deux laughed.

Mufala pointed at the star. "Will that ... thing ... be okay left alone here?"

"It is fine," Maman Ezili assured him. "We just need to remember to feed it when we return."

"There are many gods who will eat today," Papa Bon Deux replied cryptically. "Let us be off."

They followed Mufala out of the temple, leaving Javan alone with only the sputtering torches and the sound of tiny hooves for company. Soon, he heard chariot wheels on the cobblestones. Then, silence returned again.

The air still stank of the bat thing that had invaded the temple with its presence earlier. His stomach growled again. Clambering to his feet, Javan began to ascend the stairs. His thoughts swirled. What had the enemy meant about Rogan and his daughters, Erin and Algeniz? And why had Mufala said that both Karac and Karza were waiting? Karza was dead, beheaded by Rogan off the shores of Olmek-Tikal. He pondered their words, but had no answers, other than their destination. Mufala had mentioned a river. The closest river was the Severin. He resolved to go there, vowing that what had happened to Akibeel would not happen to his uncle or his cousins.

Wodan and Rhiannon, help me, he prayed. *Let me arrive in time.*

His stomach growled again as he reached the main floor of the temple. Having read many of the scrolls of the goddess' priestesses and priests, Javan knew that food existed in the temple. To eat it would be considered blasphemy, as it was served only in communion to Rhiannon, but seeing as how his options were limited, and he was pressed for time, and Rhiannon's temple had already been perverted by sorcery, he entered the sanctuary. Javan drew his sword and looked at the smashed remains of an altar on the other side of the bloody star. Behind it was a wooden cabinet, the reliquary of the bread and wine.

As Javan crept around the edge of the star, the imprisoned

beast stepped forward from the shadows. Javan gasped. It had been tiny when he first saw it. Now it stood over two feet tall. Shrieking, it ran at Javan, but stopped short at the edge of the sigil, restrained by some invisible magic. Javan cocked his sword back, wondering if the steel in the blade would cut the demon's flesh. He decided not to find out. Slashing at it would mean possibly breaching whatever force held the monster at bay.

The creature slobbered and gibbered as Javan turned his back to it. It followed him as best it could, tracing to the lines on the floor. Passing around the star, Javan reached the cabinet and opened it up. When he saw a stale loaf of bread and a flagon of wine, his ravenous appetite won over against potential blasphemy. The creature mewled, watching him eat, but Javan's grunts of satisfaction drowned out the noise.

Finished with his meal, Javan took a deep breath and prepared to head out. He knew it would probably mean his death, but there was no courage in hiding. Rogan was in chains, and Erin and Algeniz were apparently prisoners, as well. Whatever the sorcerers had planned, it wouldn't go well for his family.

When he reached the door, Javan bowed, whispering an apology to the goddess.

He whispered one to Akibeel, as well.

The thing in the star watched him leave.

THE STONE BLOCKS ERECTED BY THE PRIESTS OF ALBION ALONG the raging banks of the river Severin had honored many gods in their time. When the sun was at different positions in the sky, it would shine on various slabs. In the center of the megalithic structure was an altar composed of a simple granite slab set on two other, smaller blocks. As they marched him around the stone monoliths, Rogan's heart sank. He beheld his daughter, Erin, tied to one of the pillars. Her strawberry blonde hair waved in the slight breeze, reminding him of her dead mother. Her younger sister, Algeniz, was tied to another pillar next to her. Both girls showed no fear—only anger.

Hundreds of people had gathered around the stones and along the riverbank. Rogan assumed they were the common folk of Albion, hoping for some entertainment. He frowned. In the distance, there were still more people gathered in the shady glens, staying out of the sunlight.

"If you have shown up to see me die," he shouted, "then I am disappointed by the turnout. But I think your disappointment will be greater than mine, before this day is done."

A spear tip pricked the skin over his ribs. Rogan started to turn, but Donas shoved him forward. Rogan smiled at his daughters as his captors forced him to kneel nearby them. He gritted his teeth, plying his strength against the men surrounding him, but their number was too many. They pushed him lower, shoving him face first into the ground. Rogan struggled, wrestling with his chains as they rolled him over and propped him up. They held his legs, arms—everything but his head. That remained free, so that he could see.

A chariot rolled up in a cloud of dust. Mufala and the two elderly wizards disembarked from it. The old man reached into the chariot and pulled out a headdress fashioned from the skull of a horned creature. It was obvious to Rogan that it wasn't the skull of a bull, but he had no clue what it could be. The sorcerer donned the headdress. Then the new arrivals greeted Rohain and Karac, bowing and performing curtsies. After that, the entire group walked over to stand before Rogan.

"Did you find his nephew," Karac asked Mufala. "The one called Javan?"

Mufala shook his head. "Not yet, but we will."

"He might try to regroup with the rebels," Maman Ezili suggested. "My babies found their location on the border, when they captured the shaman."

"We will deal with them soon enough," Rohain replied, "but blood must come first, and Javan is still free."

Karac drew his short sword and put the tip beneath Rogan's chin, raising the barbarian's head until their eyes met. "Tell us where to look for your nephew and I promise I'll make his death quick."

Erin struggled in her restraints. "Don't tell them anything, father!"

Rogan grinned. "You're going to kill me, Karac, so get it over with. You've already killed one of my sons. You have my daughters and myself. You've bewitched Rohain. What need do you have for Javan?"

"All your kin must die," Karac said. "Leaving only Rohain. Speaking of which, he has a speech to give. You might enjoy it."

The trumpeters and drum corps played a long fanfare that echoed over the river and hills. Rohain stepped up onto the stone altar, and the civilians bowed. Raising his voice, Rohain thanked them all for attending, and for their loyalty, and then gave a lengthy address about quelling any vicious rumors about his guest, the visiting King Karac. He spoke eloquently of the new bonds formed between their countries—bonds that would henceforth be honored by him legally changing his name from King Rohain to King Karza. He told them he would do this in honor of Karac's noble brother, murdered by Rogan, who—after abandoning the throne—became a murderous pirate, and had been caught reaving off Albion's coast. He told them that this naming ceremony was the custom of Karac's people, and that though it might seem strange or pagan, they must come to accept it. He said there would be other customs honored, as well, and then leered at Erin and Algeniz.

The sisters tried to shout in protest as their brother lied, but the soldiers silenced them. Rogan remained quiet, brooding. He watched his son speak, listened to his words and mannerisms, and realized they were not Rohain's. It was only then that he came to believe Karac's taunts—that his firstborn son, Rohain, was dead, and that bastard Karza had been brought back from Hell to inhabit his body. The impact of this truth felt like a hammer blow to his gut. Once it started, he allowed himself to consider Teran's death, as well as the probable fate of his daughters. Rogan would have hung his head in grief, but the guards held him tight. Instead, he opted to stare into Doran's eyes.

"You will be the first to die today," Rogan promised.

Doran sneered but said nothing.

Rohain finished his address and clambered down from the altar. He nodded at Papa Bon Deux and then stood beside Karac, grinning down at Rogan.

"Is there anything of my son left inside you?" Rogan asked, his voice thick.

"No," Karza answered with Rohain's mouth. "Karac and I are your last two surviving sons."

"I hear from Rohain occasionally," Papa Bon Deux said, walking past Rogan. "I listen as his spirit cries out in torment. The sound brings me comfort."

"I promised Doran he would be the first to die today," Rogan said, "but Wodan willing, you will be second."

The wizard chortled. "There are worse things than dying. What you are about to behold, for example. That will leave you wishing you had died first."

Suddenly, Rogan saw a sight that filled him with dread. Three warriors seized Erin, unchaining her from the great standing stone. She fought, kicking and shouting as they carried her to the stone altar and tied her down. One of the soldiers reared back as her fingernails raked his face, but another punched her in the jaw, and Erin went limp. Rogan's pulse raced. Screaming, he fought against his captors, but more men rushed over and added to the dogpile. He drew breath to struggle again, but held it when the tip of a spear pressed into the soft hollow of his throat. Rogan's eyes followed the weapon's shaft up to its holder. Mufala grinned down at him.

"All of your line will die today, Rogan," Karza said, "with the exception of my brother and I, of course. But move again, and you'll go before your daughters."

Testing the truth of his words, Rogan twitched. The spear head immediately pricked his flesh. If he moved so much as another inch, it would tear his throat open.

Mufala laughed at his distress.

"You'll be third," Rogan whispered, his voice hoarse.

Papa Bon Deux strode over to Erin and raised his hands high. He turned in a circle, pausing to stare in each of the four directions of the compass, and then turned back to Erin again. A soldier stepped forward and handed him a curved blade. Rogan lay powerless, his gorge rising, his eyes burning with tears of rage, as the priest raised the blade over his head.

"Father," Erin cried, "I love you."

He tried to call out to her, to say the words he was unaccustomed to speaking, but Mufala leaned into the spear shaft, and his declaration to his daughter came out as a rasp.

Donas leaned close to Rogan's ear, and whispered, "This is all just for show, you know? There is no naming ritual. They're just using that as an excuse to butcher your family in front of the commoners."

Rogan glared at him, swearing silently that he would indeed be the first.

"Oh, Damballah," Papa Bon Deux intoned. "Accept this sacrifice, god of gods! Smile on your servants, and bless this naming rite. No matter where they may be, of such a great god! Know that we offer four sacrifices this morning. Rogan, his daughters Erin and Agenize, and the life that grows inside of Erin, fathered by her brother ..."

Rogan gasped.

"Accept these lives as supplication and bless your new king, Karza, the man who will grant you greater glories for the entire world! Grant us this, oh great god Damballah!"

The curved blade fell and Rogan's sanity fell with it. In his blind rage, he felt his soul fall to pieces and vanish as his daughter, and bastardized grandchild, perished. Unsure if it was the sound of the blade's action or his imagination, Rogan swore he heard an infant gasp. He shook, screaming, eyes wide, as Papa Bon Deux made grand designs in the bloody gore on the altar, laughing as he did so. Algeniz thrashed in her chains, wailing for her father to do something as her sister was butchered. The wizard motioned to the nearby group of soldiers. They came forth, brandishing short blades to dismember Erin, removing select pieces, and laughing as they did so. Most of the watching populace seemed to cringe and shy away from what was happening, but a few surged closer.

"You bastards," Rogan moaned. "You fucking bastards!"

Karac and Karza looked down at him, smiling.

"Indeed," Karac said. "Your bastards."

The warriors cleared away from the blood-drenched altar, and Rogan saw that there was nothing of Erin left atop the slab. What remained had dribbled down over the sides.

"Bring the other girl," Papa Bon Deux ordered.

Rogan groaned, helpless, as tiny Algeniz was stripped and tied down in the bloody gore of her sister. She wailed, fighting against her captors with even more ferocity than Erin had mustered, but she was no match for them.

"This one has spirit," Maman Ezili cackled. "She fights like her older sister did. I suppose we should expect no less from the daughters of Rogan."

The comment inspired a sudden memory for Rogan—captured by slavers when just a boy, he'd fought his way free. One of the slave masters had made a similar observation regarding his lineage. This thought stirred up another, and suddenly, Rogan understood what his father had meant when he spoke of what existed in their souls. They were barbarians. They fought with their guts ... not their heads. He was thinking too much. He was *feeling* too much. And his family was being slaughtered as a result. He forced his body to relax, letting his muscles go limp. As he'd hoped, his captors mistook it for resignation, and their hold on him loosened just a tiny bit.

"I will see you soon, father," Algeniz cried, her voice firm and fearless. "Wodan will accept us both."

Papa Bon Deux raised the knife. Donas and the other warriors loosened their grip a bit more, focused intently on the altar. Mufala's eyes were on the mock ceremony, as well. Rogan curled his foot around Donas's ankle and yanked, knocking him off balance. Surprised, Mufala reared back. With the weight of the spear tip no longer at his throat, Rogan turned his head to one side and bit down on a captor's arm, grinding his teeth together. He jerked his head back, and then—with a mouthful of flesh and blood—shifted his weight forward. It still didn't break their grip, but it confused them for a brief moment and left the soldiers scrambling. He spat the grisly morsel into the face of another soldier, who reeled away. Taking advantage of their confusion, Rogan slammed his head forward, laughing as he heard a nose crunch beneath the force. A recovered Mufala jabbed the spear at his head, but Rogan dodged the blow, and the weapon impaled another soldier instead.

Suddenly, Rogan's arms and shoulders were free of their grasp. He kicked both legs, breaking loose from the rest of the horde, and clambered shakily to his feet. As the warriors surged toward him, he quickly looped the chain, tying his hands together around Donas's neck.

"I made you a promise, cocksucker."

And then he kept it. The traitor's neck snapped with an audible pop. Donas went limp. Instead of dropping the body, Rogan used it as a shield, fending off Mufala's spear thrusts and a flurry of blades. He moved backward, desperately trying to avoid being flanked and surrounded. Instead of glancing at his daughter, he remained focused on his attackers.

"Kill him," Karza screamed. "Bring him down!"

The soldiers paused, recovering from the initial surprise. Reverting back to their training, they fanned out and approached slowly, jabbing and feinting, trying to catch Rogan off guard. The old barbarian growled, dragging Donas with him as he tried to retreat. He backed into a standing stone, and his enemies pressed forward. With his hands still bound and no weapon to wield,

Rogan realized that there was no way he could escape. Defeat was certain. All that mattered now was how he died.

"Come on, you fuckers!" He spat on the ground. "I'll take as many of you with me as I can!"

He prepared for death, wondering who would be there to greet him first—his loved ones or his enemies. The latter far outnumbered the former.

From the crowd bolted a robed figure, stabbing two soldiers in the kidneys from behind. This mystery individual moved on, slaying two more of Karac and Karza's men with a slash across their throats before they knew what was happening. In no time, the robed figure reached the inner circle.

Seeing that his king was in peril, Mufala turned toward them. In that moment, Rogan tossed Donas's corpse at the approaching attackers, knocking them to the ground. Then he leaped at Mufala, closing the distance between them before the warrior could raise his spear. Rogan put his fists together, covered in loops of chain, and struck Mufala with an uppercut, breaking his jaw at the chin.

"I promised you third," Rogan grunted. "No harm in being second, though."

As Mufala warbled a gurgling shriek, Rogan grabbed the gory bits extending from the injured man's maw and yanked hard, ripping his lower jawbone from his face. Spinning, he dodged a swinging sword blow and jabbed the splintered jawbone into the new attacker's eye.

The man from the crowd stabbed hearts and kicked groins, dropping the onrushing soldiers who were intent on protecting their king. He made his way around the altar, trying to reach Papa Bon Deux. The wizard scrambled out of the way, fleeing toward the chariots, and leaving Algeniz attended by only four gaping soldiers. Karac and Karza shouted in frustration as Maman Ezili ran after him. Their anger increased as their guards formed a circle around them, trying to hustle them away from the fight.

Rogan didn't know who this unexpected ally was, but he was

grateful for their intervention. Seeing the confusion and dismay in the expressions of his enemies gave him a jolt of savage happiness. With a barbaric howl that echoed off the megalithic columns, Rogan scooped up a fallen warrior's short, curved blade and ran toward the altar. His guttural yell frightened two of the soldiers, who turned and fled, abandoning their positions. This allowed the stranger an opportunity to cut Algeniz's bonds. Nodding his thanks, Rogan slashed the third soldier across the chest, cleanly slicing off a pectoral muscle through the thin armor plating.

Algeniz seized her opportunity, jamming her long nails into the eyes of the last man guarding her. As he screamed, gripping his bleeding sockets, Rogan lopped his head from his shoulders and jumped onto the altar, pulling the girl to her feet. Karza and Karac broke free from their phalanx of guards and charged the altar, weapons drawn. Father and daughter turned as one to face their enemies.

"You know he's not your brother?" Rogan asked. "He's not Rohain."

Narrowing her eyes, Algeniz nodded. "I know."

The two of them simultaneously launched themselves from the altar, surprising the usurpers. Algeniz stomped Karza's right foot, driving her bare heel down and tripping him, while Rogan dropped his blade and swung the loops of the chain up, connecting with Karac's groin. Karza fell face first into the dirt. The air whooshed from his lungs. Karac's eyes bulged as he fell backwards, unconscious. Dozens of enraged soldiers rushed toward them.

The mysterious ally was seized by two men, but eluded them by discarding his robes.

"Cousin Javan," Algeniz gasped.

"Focus, girl," Rogan warned.

Algeniz circled behind the altar as Karza clambered to his feet. Unable to reach his discarded weapon, Rogan did the same. As Javan reached them, the soldiers and Karza closed the gap. Rogan kicked over the altar, slick with his daughter's innards. The attackers jumped back out of the way.

Algeniz grabbed her father by the chains. "Come on!"

"She's right, sire," Javan urged. "There are too many!"

They fled. Exhausted and sick to his stomach from adrenalin, Rogan allowed them to lead him to the river. They leaped into the rushing water. Algeniz retained her grip on Rogan's chains as the churning water knocked them about. Javan swum toward them and helped her right the almost unconscious barbarian.

"We have to go back," Rogan gasped. "We have to kill them all ..."

Arrows and spears split the water around them. A throwing axe landed far short. And then the rushing current sped them around a sharp bend, and away from the standing stones. The force pushed them beneath the surface. Rogan felt the cold seep into his bones. Recovering his senses, he held his daughter up for air, and then bobbed back up himself. Javan emerged a few feet away, and managed to latch on to Rogan's chains. The three of them clung together, trying desperately to stay afloat.

"This is madness," Rogan sputtered. "We cannot swim across!"

"Who said we would?" Javan squealed. "The trick will be ...not getting crushed on the rocks!"

In moments, they were far down the river and heading toward another bank. Rogan tried to remember the geography of the area. He then remembered that up ahead was a waterfall that emptied into a lagoon which fed various rivers and lakes.

"The rocks might be a blessing," Rogan shouted.

He then did something that he rarely engaged in anymore. Rogan prayed. He prayed to Wodan, knowing the god of his father seldom cared for mortals and their activity. He knew Wodan had given him strength at birth. He prayed that Wodan would give him that blessing now ... and very quickly.

In the distance, he heard the waterfall's roar.

CHAPTER 10
THE WAY OF THE GODS

With Javan and Algeniz clinging to him, Rogan used the rocks as a buffer to slow their progress. He took the brunt each time the water slammed him into one. Battered and bruised, he relied on Javan to keep them afloat in between such episodes. Their pace was slowed enough that the plunge proved not as deadly as he had feared. They fell in a deep swell between a series of rocks acting almost like breaks, which further slowed their progress. After this, the current became much calmer. Exhausted, Rogan conceded to Javan and let the youth guide them to the forest-lined shore.

Once out of the water, they collapsed, gasping for breath and tending to their wounds as best they could with no gear or equipment. Javan's bow and sword had been lost during their plunge into the river, and his quiver was empty. Rogan tried to get his bearings by the sun, but his weariness made it difficult. Javan estimated they were somewhere in the forests between the states of Hickerson to the west and Solow to the northeast.

"We have to go back," Rogan insisted. "I will slay every one of them."

"In time, sire," Javan aid. "First, we need to seek the cover of the trees. They'll be looking for us all along these riverbanks. We must find a place to shelter and plan our revenge."

"But where?" Rogan asked. "Where is a good place to seek refuge? Where can Rohain ... Karza ... not reach? Hickerson is large and expansive, but there is nowhere to hide in that outer realm. And Solow? The populace prefers wrestling to fighting. They'll crumble beneath a military advance. We should just march back now and kill as many of them as we can."

Algeniz crawled to her father's side and hugged him. Rogan returned the embrace, but his gaze remained on the shoreline. Then, almost gently, he lowered his head and nuzzled her hair.

"You fought well back there."

"Thank you, father. Erin ..."

"Best not to think about it." He picked her up and rose to his feet. Then he placed her back on the ground at his side. "Javan is right. We should go. The forest will offer us some protection."

"From dogs and search parties," Javan agreed, "but not from Papa Bon Deux's sorcery."

"I wonder about that," Rogan said, as they limped toward the tree-line. "They were unable to find you after your escape from the throne room. Something was protecting you from his sight."

"Rhiannon be praised," Javan replied.

"If it was her," Rogan muttered. "Right now, we need all the help we can get."

"In her temple ..." Javan's expression fell. "I blasphemed. I had no choice. I was hungry and ..."

"We all do things we don't want to do, boy. Do you think I wanted to watch Erin die? Sometimes we have no choice."

"Yes, sire." The youth struggled for a moment to regain his composure. After a deep breath, he said, "If Solow and Hickerson are out, perhaps we could travel east?"

"If we head east," Algeniz reminded them, "we will cross into Morrisland. That may not be the friendliest of places."

"You speak kindly," Rogan grumbled. "Morrisland is a realm of ass-goblins and dwarves that fancy goats, my dear. There is nothing worth killing, fucking, or puking on there, and the people are so stunted that we could not hide behind them."

"That's what my school lessons tell me," Algeniz agreed. "They say that land is full of little trolls."

"So, your teachers are doing their job," Rogan muttered. "At least that is something."

"They were, until Rohain ... I mean Karza, had them all killed. But I can get my education elsewhere. I hear many things in the palace. Most talk freely in front of me because I am just a child to them. They take me for granted."

Rogan grunted. "They do that to me as well, girl. I am old. They look past the old and the very young, smug and overconfident in their youth. They thought me an old dog ready to just roll over and die. They will learn the error of their ways. I still have my balls."

As they jogged into the shadowed woods, Algeniz looked back in the direction of Albion. "They must die, father. All of them."

"They will, girl. Badly. Still, we cannot kill them alone. I say we head north, toward the higher lands, and the Pryten wilderness, and whatever forces Thyssen is supposed to be gathering. The villagers there are at least a more exclusionary folk. They will not accept that monster masquerading as Rohain as easy as these civilized city folk have."

Javan nodded. "If we muster an army for invasion, the less tangled plains in that region will fit a consolidated force."

Rogan pondered that. "If Andraste is true to her words, I wager her folk and the Troglodytes could attack from anywhere. I wish I knew what Boone was planning."

Javan's expression darkened again. As they made their way deeper into the forest, he told them what had befallen Akibeel. Rogan cursed the news, but showed no other emotion.

"We will add his name to the list of those to be avenged."

"Aye," Javan agreed.

After an hour, they paused to catch their breath. While Javan hunted for berries and nuts, Rogan tried unsuccessfully to break his chains. Soon, they heard baying of hounds. The three jumped to their feet and ran on, staying ahead of the search parties, navigating through the forests and open fields. Algeniz had no trouble keeping up. Her thin legs stabbed like a leaping fawn, but she proved more sure footed than a tiger in her journey. At times, her father let the girl ride his back. The landscape echoed with the sounds of dogs, horses, and men.

"He will never give up," Algeniz said.

"I know," Rogan replied. "But we will find help. The entire kingdom cannot be sheep! We did such great things here."

Algeniz held her bottom lip in her teeth for a few moments. "Are we really going to the Pryten Wilderness?"

"Yes," Rogan told her. "We will cut through the marshes and then into the Pryten wilderness."

She sighed. "Perhaps they will not search into such a savage place."

"That," Rogan agreed, "and also because we have friends and allies there."

Algeniz flinched. "But I thought—"

"Forget everything you thought you knew, girl. Things have changed."

As they continued on, Rogan thought of Albion's high society. How would the gentry change their life, under this new rule? Little, if their behavior so far was any indication. They swapped one brute with a crown for another.

They emerged from a grove of pine trees and tipped along a marshland, certain that no horse could travel in such a soggy path. No creatures assaulted them, but many bugs did arise and light on their skin. The sound of their steps, hard breathing and the rattle of Rogan's chains kept rhythm. Occasionally, Javan glanced at the sky through the breaks in the treetops, searching for winged creatures, but there were none, aside from sparrows.

Algeniz wiped the sweat off her brow. "I am not yet prepared to die, father. I said I was, back on that altar, but I lied. You will kill these men so I can get the time I need. If I die before then, my shade will haunt this land for eternity. I do not think the gods want that."

The old warrior said nothing. Her words were a cross between childish bravado and earnest blood anger.

"Father, what does your heart of hearts want?"

"My own son dead," Rogan seethed. "Or, at least the thing that used to be my own son. If Albion is that fickle to follow this dark butcher, perhaps it isn't worth saving. I will die before I let that bastard go on breathing, though. I would do no less to a dog."

"Maybe," Javan suggested, "we are not supposed to save them. "Maybe this is simply the gods' way of telling us who our friends are."

Rogan frowned. "If so, then their humor is not appreciated."

Hours passed and they cleared the marshland, emerging at a farming hamlet near the twisting, shallow Renraw River. A hunched over, thin, repugnant old man stood by a series of smoldering steel grates near the edge of his disused pasture. Each of the grates held a blackened pile of bones and dying embers. As they drew nearer, the wind shifted. All three grimaced. The man smelt of feces, sweat and smoke. Both of his eyes were nearly covered with cataracts. One gnarled hand clutched a rusty short sword.

He nodded at Rogan. "I've been waiting for you."

"You have?"

"My time is past and my family is gone. A madness came upon my boy. He read too much of the black arts. Possessed by a hovering spirit from afar, he slew his mother and sisters. I had to strike him down. It is a terrible thing when you must face the fact that your son is something the world can do without."

Rogan frowned, not sure of the old one's intent. Algeniz clenched her fists, moving to strike the man, but Rogan gave her a disproving look. Javan stood at attention, hands behind his back.

"There is naught left in this world for me," the farmer continued. "The world is infested with shadows and it grows shoddier day by day."

Algeniz spoke gently as her manner softened. "We need ..."

The old man nodded and gestured at his barn. "There are smith's tools in the building. Free yourself and take a mount. I see more than you think."

Rogan looked at the barn. Sigils and glyphs had been painted on it to ward off evil.

"Old man, we are—"

"The last people I will ever see. I am to assist you, and then leave this place."

They moved toward the barn and heard a strange noise behind them. When they turned, the old man was gone. Algeniz moved to look for him, but Javan and Rogan pulled her back.

"There is magic afoot here," Javan explained. "If what I suspect is true, then it is best we don't go seeking more of it out."

Nodding reluctantly, she ran to the clothes line and pulled off a well-worn brown dress and a scarf. Quickly, she donned leggings and slippers waiting in a basket nearby. She tied her hair back and went to assist Javan. In minutes, they'd smashed Rogan's bonds on the anvil. Inside the barn, they found a few short swords, daggers and two strong horses.

Still keeping clear of the roads, they took the horses and headed north-west. Javan looked in the sky often, but it remained clear.

"Sire," Javan whispered. "Surely you have heard the campfire story of Wodan appearing as a blacksmith or a wayfaring stranger to those of his children he blesses?

Rogan didn't look at him. "I have."

Javan glanced back at the direction of the farmer house. "Just wondering if we should give a prayer of gratitude?"

"You offer up something in thanksgiving, Javan. I'm about prayed out for one lifetime."

FOR THREE DAYS THEY TRAVELED, SKIRTING THE EDGE OF TOWNS and villages, staying away from populated areas and sleeping in caves and thickets. Javan hunted and Rogan speared fish. They ate their meals raw.

As the sun began to set on the third day, Javan said, "Cramond, the plains of Thule and the northern edges of the Pryten wilderness are near. If Boone and Andraste are still where we left them ...?"

"Then we should be with them before nightfall," Rogan replied. "Remember how easily you and I travelled from Boone's encampment to the capitol city? If only we had been able to go that way again. We wouldn't have spent the last three days romping around this stinking—"

His words were cut short as he was knocked from his steed by a bolo. Algeniz, who had been riding behind her father, fell off the horse as the surprised animal reared backward. Javan was removed from his mount a second after. Before they could rise, a voice called out.

"Slowly," a voice cautioned. "On your feet. Make any attempt to resist or attack and we'll cut you down. There are a dozen bows pointed at you."

They did as commanded. Javan and Rogan choked under the weight of the bolos, but did not reach for them. Squinting, Rogan peered into the dwindling light, trying to see their attackers.

"You can take the bolos off," a second voice, deep and craggy, said. "Then tell me who you are. You're not Prytens. I'd like to know where your loyalty lies before I cut out your heart and read it for myself."

Rogan undid the bolo and drew himself up to his full height, puffing out his chest.

"I am Rogan, son of Jarek, the Kelt."

At this, a murmur went through the shadowed crowd. A towering man in rusty chain mail and oiled buckskin stepped forward into the light. He gripped a hammer in his right hand. With his left, he stroked his long beard, playing in the ivory curls.

"Aye." He laughed. "I know who you are, you ugly prick. If not for me, you would never have gained the throne of Albion."

BRIAN KEENE & STEVEN L. SHREWSBURY

Rogan smiled broadly. "Thyssen, you bastard. Glad my luck is changing."

Javan gasped, and then gave a slight bow. "It is you, sir. I thought to never see you again."

"Nor I you," Thyssen replied. "When Boone told me of yer fool mission, I thought you'd run off with your uncle to your death. I see you fell off that horse with no broken bones. I am impressed. Still, we got the drop on you."

"Do you want a prize for catching an old man and two kids?" Rogan joked. "Give me wine, you son of a bitch, before I bash your fucking head in."

"Ever the statesman," Thyssen grunted. "Come. I would sit by the fire tonight and drink with both my sons, and my friend. This may be the last time we ever do so."

CHAPTER 11

FLY BY NIGHT

After a full night and following day's rest in camp, Rogan, Javan, and Algeniz had recovered from their ordeal. All three of them spent most of that time asleep, finally emerging after the sun had gone down on the second evening, ravenous and thirsty and eager for news. Boone had seen to it that they were equipped with new clothes, armor, and weapons. For security, no campfires were lit, but the moon was bright, and the camp was well-lit as a result. As they stretched and looked around, Zenata approached Javan and told him it was time for a long-overdue talk. Rogan suppressed a laugh when he saw the expression on his nephew's face. It reminded him of a cowering dog who knows it is in trouble.

"Don't stray too far," Rogan advised his nephew. "These woods are full of Troglodytes. And for Wodan's sake, don't let Andraste see the two of you sneaking off."

"Let her," Zenata said. "If she confronts us, I can finally kill her."

"Enough of that," Rogan warned. "We need her. The Prytens have a part to play in all this."

The two wandered off into the shadows. Rogan and his

daughter joined Boone, Thyssen, Andraste, and Xuxan for a meal in the center of the encampment. After a while, Andraste and Algeniz wandered off to talk.

"General," Rogan said to Thyssen, "I see that you have met my newest daughter."

"Yes." Thyssen chewed a mouthful of rabbit and glowered at Andraste. "I think you should get a hog's reward and have a band placed about your nut sack. This world needs no more of your blood."

Rogan's eyes narrowed. He blinked away visions of Teran and Erin's fates.

"You know what she wants?"

Thyssen nodded. "That is this little bitch's idea of a plan? Boone told me. To throw Albion into the dark ages and watch it burn? It makes me weep to think on it, no matter how angry I am at the general population."

"Perhaps it's what Albion deserves now," Rogan said. "Algeniz and I discussed something similar on our journey here."

"That's yer grief talking."

"No," Rogan argued. "The time for mourning. That time will be after all of the blood is finished spilling in this affair."

"We need the Prytens, General," Boone said.

Thyssen glared at him and Rogan both. "But it's my land, my home from my birth. To destroy it and exterminate all of the folk ..."

"If you refuse her aide, what will you do?" Rogan asked. "Run vainly into the jaws of death? We have not the men for such a war."

Thyssen shrugged. "Piss on her and her ghouls. Better to die as I lived than to live in a dark realm of evil or serve it by force."

Rogan watched Andraste and Algeniz giggling as they talked. His first instinct was to drag his youngest daughter away from the Pryten Queen, but then he reminded himself that she had just seen her older sister butchered. Maybe this was something she needed. He turned to Thyssen, Boone, and Xuxan.

"Long ago, you hired me out to be in your army to overthrow

evil men in control of Albion. A corrupt and dark family controlled the so-called civilized folk then."

"I remember." Thyssen nodded.

"You convinced me that Albion, the shining ideal of the world, was in danger of falling. So then, you made me the king of the great, unsullied kingdom, the example of what goodness should be. My strength made sure it endured and fear of my sword kept all takers away."

"I remember," Thyssen repeated. "I was there, you fucking monkey. What's yer point?"

"Once again, these folk of Albion have fallen into backward ways. They are at peace and lazy. Maybe the world doesn't deserve this heady ideal you envision. If all they do is evil as soon as the sword is dropped? What good is the twig of peace in the mouth of a dove unless the bloody sword is in the clutches of a raven behind it?"

Thyssen sighed. "I see that time spent wandering the world with my youngest son has worn off on you. When did you become a damned philosopher?"

"Javan is a smart lad," Rogan said. "And perhaps barbarism is the natural state of mankind, after all. Perhaps humanity deserves no better of a fate than screwing in the mud and eating each other's flesh raw."

"You say all of the comers of Albion deserve to die?" Thyssen's face grew red.

"Why do you think they deserve to live?"

Andraste wandered over to rejoin them, leading Algeniz by the hand.

"I see why mother adored you so, father," Andraste quipped.

"Shut up, girl." Rogan took a big swig of wine.

"Where is the vial of ash I gave you?"

Rogan gritted his teeth. "Albion. Taken along with the rest of my things. But Tancorix is already dead. Why would it bother me?"

"Why indeed?" Andraste asked, her voice reflective and knowing.

"Rogan," Thyssen said. "I stand with you on this, to my demise. I know there is great death to be dealt. I respect you. I owe you my life, that's why your girls aren't my wenches."

Before Rogan could respond, Javan and Zenata ran out of the forest and dashed over to them.

"A force is coming." Javan gasped for breath. "Flying the flag of Albion."

Unmoved, Thyssen muttered, "I don't care what flag they're flying—the Albion military is here in this camp."

"They fly a banner of truce," Zenata said.

"My folk have sunk back to hug the forest," Andraste replied, "but your army spreads out to meet them."

"As they should." Thyssen upended his empty canteen and frowned.

"Marching wine," Xuxan told him, "is always the first victim of any war."

Thyssen clapped the sea captain on the shoulder. "I like you."

"The flag of truce, eh?" Rogan rose to his feet. "Let us go meet them. Algeniz, you will stay here."

The little girl balled her fists. "I will not."

"I don't have time to argue with you, girl. You will stay here, or you will wish you had."

They followed Javan and Zenata down a twisting path, through the dense forest. Emerging onto a hilltop, they looked down into a valley, where two dozen cloaked warriors waited. Moonlight reflected off the royal colors of Albion on fluttering silken banners.

"Bah," Thyssen snarled. "Only a few are from Albion proper! The rest are invaders."

Rogan slashed through the air with his fist. "And they come to speak truce terms with Thyssen? Or is this a ruse to determine if Algeniz, Javan and myself are here?"

"Or perhaps both," Boone suggested.

Thyssen turned to Xuxan. "Have yer men and the Kennebeck folk join Andraste's forces in the forest. I don't want these fuckers kenning to our true numbers. Zenata, you go with him and let yer people know. Tell my soldiers and Boone's company to get up here on the double."

Nodding, Xuxan and Zenata ran back toward the camp to carry out his orders.

A figure broke from the delegation and proceeded up the hill, riding atop a black horse. Armored and armed, he carried a white flag on the end of a long spear. As he drew nearer, Rogan and Javan both gasped.

"Karac!"

"Are you sure?" Thyssen asked. "My eyes don't have the same strength as my prick."

"It is him," Boone confirmed.

"Then he shall die," said a small voice behind them.

The group turned to see Algeniz standing there clutching a dagger.

"Damn it, girl," Rogan cursed in frustration. "You will mind me!"

Andraste and Thyssen both laughed.

"I would say she already does mind you, father," Andraste quipped. "Or, to be more specific, she has a mind like you."

Shaking his head, Rogan stared down at his daughter. "You are to stay behind us. If blood is shed, do your best to shed more of theirs than your own. Understand?"

Algeniz nodded. "Yes, father."

Rogan turned back to watch Karac approach. "Why so few men in the peace party?"

Thyssen rubbed his gray beard. "Perhaps the truce offer is genuine. Maybe he plans to offer me a deal for yer head and a position in the government."

Rogan raised an eyebrow. "An attractive position?"

"I'm just the right age to sit on my ass for the rest of my days," Thyssen replied.

"Lucky for me, you are a cantankerous old prick that still wants to fight."

Snorting, Thyssen thumbed the handle of his sword. "Lucky for you, that my hemorrhoids keep me standing up a great deal. Otherwise, I'd sell your aged ass down the river."

"Father," Javan whispered. "Uncle. The cloaked figures below. I think I have seen them before."

"Tell me later," Thyssen said, stepping forward to meet Karac. "That's far enough."

Karac stopped his horse and surveyed each of them. His eyes widened in surprise when he saw Rogan, Javan and Algeniz. Then he turned back to address Thyssen.

"I am Karac, brother and general of King Karza of Albion, the last two male heirs of King Rogan."

Thyssen raised both eyebrows. "Oh yes? I've heard of you. I've heard you fuck sheep."

"I've not come to trade quips. I am instructed to inform you that King Karza is the first from Rogan's thighs and rightful heir to the throne of Albion."

"You think a blood line insures anything in this world?" Thyssen asked. "Rogan's father wasn't king of anything! He was a simple smith."

Karac shrugged. "The political structures of Kittim, Zimbabwe, and Kemet have already accepted our legal right. The war is over."

Andraste stepped forward, hands on her hips. "What does that matter to me? You come to make palaver with General Thyssen, but you are in my land now, uninvited. The Pryten people will not react kindly to such an affront. You say your war is over? I say it is just beginning."

"Who am I addressing?" Karac asked.

"I am Andraste, queen of the Prytens. Conquest is the way of the world. If you want a throne, kill the king and take it. But you are laboring to be legitimate, as you say in the civilized world? When you rode out of Albion and crossed into our home land, you exited the civilized world. You are in my world now."

Karac bowed. "That is why we fly a flag of truce, my lady."

Rogan laughed. "She's no lady."

Ignoring him, Karac turned to Thyssen again. "General Thyssen, there's no need for harsh feelings with us. Come back and designate our fighting forces and all of the Imperial dreams you want will be fulfilled."

"A tempting offer," Thyssen admitted. "A cushy job in my elder years? Hmm. Could I really lead troops at my age?"

Before Karac could answer, Thyssen and Boone's men marched out of the forest, their weapons on display. They formed ranks behind the general and stared, unblinking, at the invaders.

Karac motioned to them with a sweep of his hand. "You inspire everyone. That's more of a weapon than steel, at times."

Thyssen shrugged. "I've heard tell a million blacks march here from the south to support yer revolution. Would these men obey an old man like me? Would they have the courage to overwhelm the Pryten wilderness and drive these vile savages into the sea? Would they show fear at their Druid gods? Would they go north into Thule, cross the tundra or freeze in their tracks when the temperature bit their noses?"

"We can see."

"Tempting, but I think not. I'd rather take my chances here with Rogan and Queen Andraste."

"You owe Rogan little," Karac said.

"I'm standing right here, dog," Rogan said. "You can damned well speak to me."

Still ignoring him, Karac continued. "Follow King Karza, a true warrior, not a high bred politician. He is more like Rogan in his youth than this doddering old pretender can ever hope to be."

Thyssen nodded. "I have respected your flag of truce, and I've given you my answer. Is there anything else?"

"Very well." Karac sneered. "But know this. If we cannot win their hearts, they can be given to our god. One by one, they will all knuckle under or die. We vastly outnumber you."

Rogan glanced at the expressions of Thyssen and Boone's soldiers. Many of them seemed confused and frightened by Karac's threat, and gripped their weapons tight. Grimacing, he drew his sword and stepped in front of Thyssen.

"One by one?" Rogan asked. "Then start with me, if you can."

Karac smiled. "I have taken you once already, old man. But to do so with your forces behind you? You must think me a fool."

Rogan nodded at the cloaked figures standing at the bottom of the hill. "You have your own warriors down yonder."

"Indeed, I do, father. Indeed, I do ..."

Karac's smile grew wider. He raised his hand and motioned to his troops. At his signal, the two dozen members of the delegation cast off their long cloaks, revealing themselves not to be warriors or soldiers, but something else entirely. They were very tall, with elongated feet and hands, and drooping jaws. Their skin was rippled and armored, like some obscene cross between a bat and a crocodile. At first, Rogan thought each of them was wearing a leather backpack, but then the bulky appendages unfurled into wings.

"Arise," Karac shouted. "Arise, children of Damballah!"

Shrieking, the creatures took flight.

Both Rogan and Thyssen swore simultaneously.

"Wodan!"

"I tried to tell you," Javan said. "I have seen them before, in Rhiannon's temple."

"These are the things that abducted Akibeel," Boone shouted. "To arms!"

"Fire," Thyssen ordered.

A hail of arrows battered the creatures but had no noticeable impact. The beasts didn't slow.

Rogan's attention was focused on the enemies in the air. Laughing, Karac lowered his spear and reared back, taking aim at the barbarian's chest. As he threw it, Thyssen dived to his side, shoving Rogan out of harm's way. The spear nicked his armor. Thyssen rolled off Rogan and sprang to his feet, throwing a slender hunting knife at Karac. The blade glanced off the black invader's iron breast plate. Before Karac could react, Rogan spider-crawled forward and grabbed his fallen sword. Karac drew a curved sword from his scabbard. Before he could get it free, Rogan, his face a mask of brutal fury, slashed forward, chopping the hind leg off of Karac's mount. Blood sprayed, bathing both men. Screeching, the horse toppled over, sending Karac tumbling from the saddle.

Thyssen and Boone's archers ceased firing as the creatures swooped down upon them. As the inhuman things descended into their midst, the soldiers opted for axes, spears and swords instead. One monster grabbed Thyssen's shoulders with its clawed feet and threw the old general to one side. Another dropped on Rogan, clutching his shoulders, swatting at him with pointed wings. Rogan sliced through the membrane of the creature's wing, but a second beast seized him, talons sinking deep into the thick muscle of Rogan's thigh. Claws raked across his ribs, slashing through his chainmail armor. Bellowing in pain, Rogan slashed at his attacker. His sword glanced off the thing's hide. He then probed for a heart with his dagger, but found none.

As a third creature swooped in to attack, Boone rushed forward, wielding a battle-axe, and managed to catch the beast on top of Rogan with a back-swing. The blade didn't cleave the flesh, but the momentum of the blow caused the creature to release Rogan. Rogan jumped to his haunches, clutching his sword, and nodded thanks.

"The wings," he yelled. "Aim for the membrane on their wings!"

As Boone waded into the fray, repeating the order, Rogan glanced around the battlefield. He saw Thyssen and Karac fighting. Their swords sparked against each other. Suddenly, the old man seemed to weaken and fell to one knee. Buying into the ploy, Karac advanced too fast. Thyssen swung his left hand up between his attacker's legs, connecting with Karac's groin. Laughing as he rose up, he slammed his horned helmet into Karac's jaw, drawing blood and stunning the man. Before Karac could recover, Thyssen lopped off his hand at the wrist. It fell to the ground, still clutching Karac's sword. Reeling, Karac staggered backward. Thyssen punched him in the face, stunning him more. He raised his sword to deliver a death blow, and then froze as a high-pitched scream rang out above them.

All heads turned skyward. Tiny Algeniz dangled in the clutches of one of the creatures. Andraste ran after her, shrieking. Javan raised his bow, sighted, and then let his shoulders sag, cursing. Stumbling, Rogan reached vainly toward the sky as they soared higher. A second later, two more creatures grabbed his arms and yanked him off the ground. His sword plummeted to the earth as he was pulled into the sky. Javan raised his bow again, but before he could fire, he too was captured. Their friends could only watch helplessly as they were flown over the trees, back toward Albion.

Karac ran back down the hillside. Seeing him escaping, Thyssen roared with rage and prepared to give chase. Before he could act, however, Andraste cried out in a shrill tongue. A moment later, a dozen Troglodytes spilled out of the forest, bounding over the stunned soldiers and leaping down the hill in pursuit. Karac glanced around wildly, and then fell to his knees, clutching his bleeding stump as the ravening Troglodytes bore down on him. Looking up at the sky, he screamed.

"Damballah!"

Then the Troglodytes were on him. Within moments, they'd reduced him to shreds of meat, scattered across the field.

As the winged creatures vanished from sight, carrying Rogan, Javan, and Algeniz with them, Boone hacked the wings off the creature that Rogan had injured. Then he began cutting into the wounds until the monster was split into pieces, dropping his blade over and over as if the blows would bring back those who had been stolen.

Thyssen wheeled on Andraste. "I thought I told you to keep those damned things in the woods?"

"They were in the woods," she countered.

"If my men have to throw in with your lot, then you keep those damned things away from us. It's not a choice. Understand?"

Andraste picked up Rogan's sword. "I think our choices are very clear now."

CHAPTER 12

LAST DAWN OVER ALBION

Rogan awoke in flight, angry at himself that he passed out, even more enraged that he couldn't see Algeniz nor Javan. The horizon glowed, indicating that the sun would soon rise. Only one of the creatures carried him now. The other must have taken off while he was unconscious. His captor flew slower, descending as they swept in over the capitol city, near to the top of the outlying homes. Rogan spied the temple of Rhiannon in the distance and recalled what Javan had said about the demon imprisoned there. Was he being taken to feed Bon Deux's pet, rather than back to the palace dungeon? Perceiving this as his possible fate, Rogan set about in planning an escape.

Getting used to the rhythm of his captor's wings and gait, Rogan wagered his weight could displace the beast if he swung himself up at the precise time. As the temple grew closer, he gauged the drop to the closest roof. Then he grabbed the creature's ankles and swung his legs up. The monster squawked in surprise. Rogan pushed off with his hands, tearing free from its clutches. The thing snatched at him, but he fell fast, impacting on the thatched roof of a domicile. He flipped in midair, but ended up taking the brunt of the fall on his left shoulder. His weight sent him crashing through the roof, but not completely onto the floor of the home. So heavy and reinforced was the thatch and boards under it, Rogan became hung up, boots still outside in the air.

Arms swaying like pendulums, Rogan cursed and tried to focus on the dim light. The hearth had lowered, but an oil lamp soon flared, held by a boy of almost ten years, who sat up on a bed mat and gaped at the hairy brute as he swung back and forth.

"Boy," Rogan ordered as he tried to work his legs free, "bring me a weapon!"

Blinking, the child leapt from the bed, obedient to the words, but paused when something slammed into the roof. Kicking and cursing, hair across his face, Rogan shouted as the roof sagged around him. More thatch spewed down, and then Rogan came loose, falling near the hearth. He groaned and growled in both pain and anger. Quick to his knees, Rogan barked again for a weapon. This time, the child didn't move, paralyzed with fear.

Staggering, happy to have something solid under his boots again, Rogan climbed to his feet and glanced around. The house was divided into three rooms. Determining that his present location contained no weapons or anything of use, he sprinted toward the next room. The creature squealed outside. Trembling, the boy trotted after Rogan.

The next room held a table and four chairs. In the corner was an oblong wooden case with a glass covering. Rogan looked at the boy and sighed. He gave the glass front a hard kick and the cover shattered. Pulling out a two-edged broadsword with his right hand, Rogan grabbed the wooden handle of another weapon and drew it out. It was a flail sporting two lines, each having a spike ball on the end. He had little time to contemplate any of the weapons, as the winged beast dropped down through the hole in the roof.

"Stay here," Rogan said.

The boy nodded, but when Rogan rushed back into the first room, the boy followed, screaming when he saw what was there.

The creature's wings scraped across the ceiling. It swiped at the terrified child with one clawed hand, but Rogan elbowed the boy in the head, sending him to the floor and out of range. Thrusting the sword, Rogan speared through the membranous wing and nailed the monster to the wall. Releasing the pommel of the broadsword, he grabbed the flail with both hands and reared back. The beast's eyes widened as Rogan whipped the double spiked balls at its cranium. Despite scoring a direct hit, the weapon did little more than knock the beast senseless. Hissing, it pawed at the sword hilt sticking out of its pinned wing and then glanced around the room, as if unsure of what to do next. Rogan swung the flail again. This time, he dented the creature's head. Encouraged, he thought of Erin and Teran and Rohain, shouting their names as he worked the flail over and over until he smelled brains. He didn't stop until the thing's pulped head ran down its broad shoulders.

Panting, Rogan turned to the stunned boy and asked, "Who are you?"

"Rogan," the child replied.

"What?"

"My name is Rogan, named after the great king my father once fought for."

"Where is your father now?"

The boy shrugged. "I don't know. It's a bad time. He's a palace guard and he drinks too much. My mother died, after the men from the south came. He spends most of his time at the inn, when not on duty."

Frowning, Rogan nodded. "Why does your father keep steel under glass? Wodan gave us steel to use, not keep on a shelf."

"He says they are old collector's items."

Grunting, Rogan wrenched the sword free from the wall. The creature's corpse slid down to the floor.

"They still work," he said. "I'll borrow them for a bit."

"My father will ask who took them. Who are you?"

"Would you believe me if I told you I was the former king of this land, Rogan, son of Jarek?"

"No," the boy admitted. "They said King Rogan escaped a few

days ago, and fled north. Only a fool would come back to Albion after that, and King Rogan was no fool."

Rogan tousled the boy's hair. "Does your father keep any wine or whiskey in this house?"

The boy showed him a cupboard where the wineskins were kept. Rogan unscrewed the end of the skin, marveling at the craftsmanship. Taking a long draw on the wine, he opened a wooden box on a shelf beneath the cupboard. Raising an eyebrow, Rogan took out a cigar bit the tip off. Then he lit the cigar from the fireplace.

"Are you in trouble?" the boy asked. "What is that monster?"

"That monster is one of my many troubles."

The boy's eyes widened. "You are King Rogan, aren't you?"

Rogan winked.

"What are you going to do?"

Rogan puffed the cigar. "What I want to do and what I can do are two different things."

"What is it you want to do?"

"Kill the world, find my friend Xuxan, and go fishing." He stood, and nodded. "Thank you for the weapons and your hospitality. Sorry about the roof."

"If you really are King Rogan, then you shouldn't be here. You'll die if they catch you."

"No," Rogan replied, walking to the door. "There's too many people I have to kill before I leave this place."

ALGENIZ WAS SURPRISED WHEN SHE AWOKE UNRESTRAINED AND not in a cell, but in her nightclothes and her bed. Two armored guards stood to either side of her door. One of them was an Albion regular whom she'd seen around the palace before the uprising. The other was one of Karac and Karza's men. Upon seeing her stir, the former opened the door and informed someone else in the corridor that the princess was awake. After the door closed again, Algeniz heard booted feet marching down the hall.

Glancing around, Algeniz studied her room. It felt strange to be there. Her toys and books and clothes seemed alien and unfamiliar. She wondered where her father was. In the dungeon? Dead already? She thought of Erin and her unborn child, sacrificed to the heathen god of Papa Bon Deux. Struggling not to cry, she turned her attention back to the guards, and slid out of bed. The floor was cold beneath her feet.

"I have to make water," she informed them.

The guards stared straight ahead, ignoring her.

Algeniz drew herself up to her full height. "I said, I have to make water!"

"You are not to leave until King Karza arrives."

"I'll piss on the floor, then."

The black guard shrugged. "And you'll clean it up ... with your tongue."

She heard echoing feet returning. Soon, the door opened and Rohain entered the room, accompanied by two warriors in royal armor. Rohain himself wore King Rogan's regalia dress armor.

Karza, she thought. *I have to remember, he's not my brother anymore. He's Karza.*

"Hello, little one."

Algeniz took a deep breath, trying very hard not to show them she was afraid. "Has my destiny finally arrived? Here to try cutting me up on the altar again?"

"I have good news for you."

"Oh, you are dying of a dreaded sickness and the worms will feast on your eyes soon?"

Karza scowled with Rohain's face.

"You said good news," Algeniz pressed. "Don't play games with me."

"I understand. You see little reason for you to still be alive. The boon of your life should make you pleased."

Algeniz looked to the window, affixed shut and secured with two recently installed cross bars. The sun rose over the city. She picked up an ivory haired doll and clutched it to her chest.

"I'm beyond usefulness to you. Sacrifice me if you must. I am too little for my womb to do you any good. If I am going to die, get it over with or get out."

"You have spirit," Karza murmured. "In time, you could produce great offspring."

"I know why you have barred the windows. It's because I would sooner cast myself out the window than produce anything more than puke for you."

"Oh, not for me. But perhaps Karac will bed you when you are of age."

"Karac's dead. I saw it myself." Algeniz stroked the doll's hair. "My Uncle Thyssen cut his hand off. He cried like an infant and ran away. Then a pack of ... things ... tore him apart."

Karza crossed the room in four quick strides and seized her by the neck. His broad fingers encircled her throat. He lifted her off the floor with one hand. Algeniz dropped the doll. Karza stomped it beneath his boot heel. Spittle flew from his lips.

"You lie."

Algeniz stared at him, unblinking and unafraid. Then, slowly, she shook her head. Karza held her there for a moment, shaking with rage. Algeniz refused to break her stare, even as her lungs began to pound. Spots danced in her vision, and she heard a roaring in her ears. Then, Karza threw her onto the bed. Fists clenched, he stood there, seething. Algeniz drew breath. Her throat felt raw.

"You do have spirit," Karza said again, his voice low and thick. "I wonder if you get that from your mother or our father? Your mother was a powerful woman to tame Rogan. It's a shame you slew her in your birth. That must've driven a wedge between you and Rogan, no?"

She glanced down at her shattered doll. "You act as if my mother was the first woman to die in child birth. Leave me alone and save your mind games for weaker children. My father was cut from his mother by my grandfather, Jarek. He was tame long enough to give me life, as well as you. If I wanted him to be a simpering wet nurse, by Rhiannon, he wouldn't be Rogan, now would he?"

"You believe you have his strength?"

"I believe I have my father's Kelt blood. I believe that I will live again, as surely as my slain siblings. Kill me, Rohain ... or Karza, and I will go back to Wodan, the god of my father. I will impart him to leave his mountain and fight your damned Damballah. I doubt if he would listen, but I would hate to get his full attention. My desire is to only direct it to you."

Karza roared with laughter. "Does Wodan watch over your father? You heard he fell to his death with the creature carrying him?"

"A better death than that of your brother, Karac." Algeniz shrugged. "If true, then it's just another adventure ended."

"Adventure?"

"That's all my father's life has been. One adventure after another, whether wandering as a boy or battling under the sword of some foreign power, he stumbled through a life filled with adventure. I'm sure to him it was fun and exhilarating to die in such a fashion. The only other thing he ever desired was to be a king."

Karza grinned. "But now I am king."

Algeniz turned toward the window again. "And you will discover what he did later in your life. The warrior's heart can only be quelled so long. Either you give in, become soft, or pretend to enjoy the politics, the Imperial advances and go hunting every beast of the field. My father was caged here. His long adventures away from Albion and visits to foreign lands were thinly disguised adventures. He sought his end. Whenever a battle came up or an adventure dawned, I knew there was a possibility he would never return. Even as a toddler, I understood him as none of my siblings. He left me a good life." Her eyes narrowed and returned to Karza. "But you have upset all of that, haven't you? Over some savage desire to be him, you have invaded my life, haven't you? You have his frame, his power and even his crown, but you cannot be Rogan. Still, you never answered my wonder."

"Why you are alive?" he asked. "Because I wished to have this talk with you first. I wished to gloat before we fed you to Papa Bon Deux's pet. I wanted you to experience your room and your things and your former life one last time before I took it all away. Now we shall go to the temple of Rhiannon!"

Algeniz swung her legs out of bed. "Whatever shall I wear?"

JAVAN STIRRED FROM UNCONSCIOUSNESS, AWARE OF SOMEONE lightly slapping his cheeks.

"Stop it, Zenata," he murmured.

"Soon everything will stop," a voice whispered. "The end is near. You must repent. But first you should be free."

Blinking, Javan opened his eyes. At first, he couldn't focus, but as his vision cleared, he saw that he was in the castle dungeon, tied to a chair with heavy ropes. A thin, scraggly, unkempt boy leaned over him, working at his knots.

"What time is it?" Javan slurred.

"After sunrise," the boy replied. "I know that because there is a little mouse that creeps through here every morning after the sun comes up. Hold still, now. These knots are tricky. The guards joked that they weren't going to waste chains on you like your uncle. They said you lacked his strength, and rope would suffice. I'm glad to hear of your Rogan's escape, by the way."

"Who are you?" Javan asked.

"My name is Jasper-Thal. Your uncle was imprisoned here with me. I watched them take him away, but I have heard he escaped and fled."

Javan's expression darkened. "He has since been captured again. Have you seen him? Do you know where he is being kept?"

Jasper-Thal shook his head. "I am afraid that until recently, I have not been clear of mind. I was sent here for being a heretic, and it made me crazy. I worship the one true God, who will soon drown this world with a great flood."

"I follow Rhiannon."

"As do many in this city." Jasper-Thal grunted, tugging at the knots. "After you were brought here, while you were still unconscious, my God sent an angel to visit me. He freed me from my chains and dissipated the fog that had crept into my head. I know you'll say that was just a dream, but I have faith."

Javan felt the ropes go slack and fall away. He shrugged out of them with some difficulty. His arms and legs felt as if they were being pricked by hundreds of needles. He wiggled them, trying to get his circulation back.

"I don't care if you are devout, touched by your deity, or just crazy," Javan said. "All that matters to me is that you helped me free myself. Now, let me see about freeing us both from this cell."

THYSSEN'S FORCES MARCHED IN ATTACK FORMATION, INTENT ON invading the city proper. The armies of Thule and Cramond had sent messages via ravens of their advance from the north.

"Let them chew on that rugged terrain," Thyssen said. "They can play with the forces Karza sends up there while we liberate the capitol."

"I want it to start," Boone said.

Thyssen frowned. "Settle yourself, soldier. You won't once it starts. This will be high butchery, not just warfare. No prisoners."

"That sounds delightful," Andraste purred.

Thyssen turned to the Pryten queen. "All of yer fighting folk and little beasty bastards better show their mettle when the time comes or we are all fucked."

She nodded. "Your kindness amazes me."

Thyssen regarded his oldest son. Boone sat up straight in his saddle, staring straight ahead as the sun rose over the hills.

"You remember how mad you got as a youth?" Thyssen asked. "When I sent Javan off to university while you joined the army?"

Boone nodded. "I do, General. I wanted an education, as well."

"Aye, you did. And you got one. Life and war are educational. Yer about to put that education to the test. Ya got the balls?"

Boone saluted. "Yes, sir."

"Good." Thyssen said. "Yer going to need them. It's gonna be a long day. We shall see the capitol before nightfall, but I reckon we'll be fighting and dying long before then."

As they rode, the clouds began to thicken and cluster overhead. Xuxan sniffed the air and glanced up at the sky.

"It's going to rain," he muttered.

"Yes," Andraste agreed. "Blood."

CHAPTER 13
THE THING IN THE TEMPLE

Javan and Jasper-Thal lurked in an alley within view of the palace. Both of them wore ill-fitting armor they had taken from the guards. Javan had also liberated a bow, arrows and a short sword from their jailers. Jasper-Thal was armed with only a dagger. In his weakened physical condition, a sword had proven too heavy for him to effectively wield. Thunder rumbled overhead and storm clouds coalesced over the city. Soon, it began to rain. Ignoring it, the two munched pilfered apples and stared at the palace towers.

"If the princess resides there," Jasper-Thal suggested, "then we should free her."

"We just escaped from the dungeon beneath it," Javan reminded him. "And as much as I want to save my little cousin, that may be impossible, even for an archer and a religious radical. By now, they have surely discovered our escape. The palace will be buzzing with guards. Rogan must be our first priority. We know he wasn't imprisoned with us. My guess is they took him to the temple of Rhiannon to feed that creature of Bon Deux's."

Jasper-Thal blanched. "I will not enter that pagan temple for your pagan king. I would surely die there!"

Javan shrugged. "We're going to die sooner or later. If you want to part ways with me now, you can. You set me free. I shall return the favor. But ... if you die in the temple, then you will see your God that much sooner, right?"

"But I can't die yet. I am too young. The angel gave me instructions. There is something I must do."

"Well then," Javan said, stalking forward, "if your deity has given you a mission, then He he won't let you die today. I just hope Rhiannon blesses me in a similar fashion."

THE TORCHES IN THE MAIN SANCTUARY OF THE TEMPLE OF Rhiannon cast Rohain's face in a savage profile. Algeniz, wearing a powder-blue gown, stood against the wall, unchained, but clutched by Maman Ezili. Papa Bon Deux hunkered down near the lower points of the blood-drawn star. Two soldiers guarded the temple entrance, wearing expressions of fear. More were stationed outside the temple, standing in the rain. Thunder rumbled, and the torches sputtered for a moment.

"Do you like my pet, little snowflake?" Papa Bon Deux asked Algeniz.

"You should get a dog," Algeniz suggested.

Maman Ezili cackled. "It will soon have enough blood to spin itself a cover and then, well, what emerges will not be confused for a dog."

"Ah," Karza said with Rohain's voice, "but dogs are ineffective in war, if loyal to a fault."

"What did you name it?" Algeniz asked, trying to sound brave.

"Names are powerful things," Papa Bon Deux answered. "Better to ask what something is called. This is called a Helvectia. It is a gift from Damballah."

Outside, the thunder boomed again. The creature in the star snorted and clattered its heavy hooves. It sniffed the air, as if its appetite had been awakened by the sight of the little girl. It stood the height of a deer, and tusks protruded from the sides of its mouth. A cluster of tentacles waved from its back, beneath two expanding wings.

"It's growing quickly," Karza observed. "What will happen after we feed it the girl?"

"It should double in size," Papa Bon Deux replied. "But we will still be able to control it, as long as the star remains intact. I am working on taming it to my will, but it is ... difficult."

Laughing, Karza turned to Algeniz. "It is a shame we have to feed you to it, Princess. What do you think? If you weren't about to die, would you carry this memory forever?"

"Not really," Algeniz said. "I'm not one for idle thoughts or bad dreams. And I'm not one for dying."

With that, the small girl lunged forward, dragging the unprepared Maman Ezili with her. The two of them crossed the bloody star, stepping over its boundaries. With all her strength, Algeniz managed to rip free from the old woman's clutches and jump back. Crying out, Maman Ezili stumbled further into the star. The creature spun toward them, seizing her with its tentacles.

"No!" Papa Bon Deux howled as Karza held him back.

Algeniz scrambled backward, and glanced around frantically, looking for a place to hide. The guards at the door rushed into the center of the room, weapons drawn, and stared in confusion and terror as Maman Ezili screamed. The beast rammed its large tusks under her collarbones and lifted Maman Ezili from the floor. Her legs kicked helplessly as the Helvectia shook her violently, ripping her apart with its arms and tentacles. Then it began to feed.

"Little bitch!" Papa Bon Deux slipped from Karza's grasp. The old wizard, mad with rage, dashed around the edge of the star. Algeniz tried to flee but he grabbed her hair and yanked her backward. Spinning, he threw her into the sigil. Algeniz bounced off the monster's left leg. The beast, still sucking the last bits of Maman Ezili from its tusks, only flinched, apparently intent on finishing its meal of the old woman.

"What are you waiting for?" Karza pointed at the girl. "Eat, you damned thing!"

Algeniz scurried backward as the beast dropped Maman Ezili's robes and focused its attention on her. She crawled out of the Helvectia's prison, cowering as the monster stalked toward her, stepping over the bloody star.

"The sigil was breached," Papa Bon Deux warned. "It is free! You have to get it back into the star and keep it there until I can recite the—"

"Just do it," Karza snapped, "or I'll feed you to this thing next and find a new wizard to serve me."

As the Helvectia reached for Algeniz, Karza jumped forward, cartwheeling past the beast and landing by Algeniz. Avoiding the tentacles, he crouched like a tiger, ready to spring. The creature stomped toward him. Karza dived low. Tentacles flailed in empty air. Standing at the star's edge, Papa Bon Deux began to chant. The beast roared. Karza cupped his arms between its legs and pulled up. Squealing, the monster flopped onto its back in the center of the star, huge jaws snapping. Karza planted both feet on the thing's belly and summersaulted back out of the trap, just as Papa Bon Deux finished his recitations. Imprisoned once again, the Helvectia went wild, thrashing and screeching.

"She's gone," Karza yelled.

"Yes." Papa Bon Deux stared at the shredded robe of his mate. "I loved her."

"Not Maman Ezili, you fool! The princess! Algeniz! She's gone!"

The wizard shook, almost catatonic. Karza motioned to the soldiers.

"Find her, or you two will feed this thing next."

Inside the star, the Helvectia aimed its tentacles upward. A gooey, white webbing spurted from the tips of its limbs. The substance wound around the beast, coating the hooves.

Outside, the rain fell harder.

ROGAN WATCHED THE GUARDS MILLING ABOUT THE ENTRANCE TO the temple of Rhiannon. The royal chariot was parked nearby, which meant that Karza was inside. Hugging the alley wall, Rogan contemplated his moves. It had been a long time since he'd had to play the role of a stealthy assassin. He recalled what Javan had told him about the thing residing in the temple. This rekindled his bloodlust to slay Bon Deux and the bastard who had stolen his son's body.

"Fuck it. No sneaking about. I'll just stick with what I know best."

Sword in one hand, flail in the other, Rogan strode forward. Water plastered his mane to his forehead and shoulders. The rain fell in sheets, almost blinding, and he was able to close the distance to the temple doors before the soldiers noticed him coming. He counted eight of them, and smiled as they drew their weapons and spread out. The tallest of them stepped forward.

"Stop where you—"

His command was cut short by Rogan's sword, which swung upward, severing the man's left hand at the wrist and then continuing on to slice through his face and cleave his jawbone. As he pulled his sword back, Rogan swatted the flail blindly in defense, inadvertently planting one of the spiked balls in the groin of another man. The soldier stood still, in agony and surprise. Rogan pulled the flail back, ripping loose the guard's manhood. The soldier collapsed to the rain-slicked courtyard, cradling the bloody ruin where his genitals had been.

The other soldiers circled in fast. Blocking a strike with his broadsword, Rogan spotted morning stars in the hands of two men. They moved to either side of him, waiting for him to extend his arms. Rogan knew the tactic well. They intended to wrap his limbs up with the long strains. When his arms were secure and pulled to their utmost, he would be easy to disarm. He'd used the same maneuver against opponents in the past. Grinning, rain streaming from his shoulders, Rogan raised his arms in invitation.

He grimaced as they attacked, crying out in mock surprise. Then, as the strains wound around his arms, he jerked both men off their feet, yanking the weapons from their grasp.

"Not today," he said. "I am not a dog to be leashed."

Dropping his weapons, Rogan swung both arms. One blow went wild, and the loop unwound from his arm, sending the morning star hurtling into the garden. The other one smashed into a soldier's head, denting the man's helmet. The man rocked back and forth. Then blood streamed down his face. He tried to speak, but toppled over face-first instead.

Gripping the morning star, Rogan bent and snatched up his broadsword. The soldiers charged, rushing him. He struck one in the forehead with the morning star, and held another at bay with the sword. As a third closed the distance between them, Rogan elbowed him in the nose. As the soldier reared backward, Rogan slashed his throat. Then, he lunged forward, pressing the attack.

Within seconds, only one soldier remained. He gaped at Rogan, mouth working silently. Then, he turned and fled, shouting the alarm. Laughing, Rogan watched him disappear down the rainy city streets.

"Let them come," he muttered. "I'll kill every man in this city."

He strode up to the temple, but before he could enter, the doors crashed open. Two soldiers rushed outside, skidding to a stop when they saw him. Karza stood behind them, his eyes wide with surprise.

"Delay him," he ordered the guards. Then, over his shoulder, he called, "Bon Deux! We have a guest."

The two soldiers attacked. Rogan parried their blows, but they pressed forward, forcing him back out into the courtyard. He saw Karza slip out the door behind them. Thinking the usurper intended to flank him, Rogan trotted backward, retreating a dozen paces. The soldiers followed. To Rogan's surprise, instead of attacking from behind, Karza jumped into the royal chariot and whipped the horses. They sped off, whinnying.

"Fuck," Rogan yelled.

The soldiers advanced, staying apart from each other. Frustrated, Rogan ran toward them, dropping at the last moment and sliding forward on the wet cobblestones. With one mighty swing, he chopped their legs out from under them, and then slid past as they fell to the ground. Clambering to his feet, Rogan looked for the chariot, but it was already gone from sight. The soldiers writhed and shrieked, their blood mixing with the puddles. Panting, Rogan walked over to them and smashed their heads in. Then he turned toward the temple and stomped through the doors.

Papa Bon Deux stood in the center of the room. Behind him was the blood-painted star that Javan had described. But Rogan saw no monster imprisoned within its confines. Instead, there was a large, white cocoon, taller than even Rogan himself.

"Well, well." Papa Bon Deux managed a weak laugh. His demeanor seemed weary and sad. "Come in out of the rain, barbarian. Close the doors behind you. That wind makes the torches sputter."

Rogan pulled the doors shut behind him—not because the wizard had commanded it, but because he didn't want the torches to be extinguished. Fighting sorcerers was bad enough. Battling them in darkness was a fool's errand. The doors boomed closed. Rogan advanced slowly, wary of a trick. He tried to remain calm, knowing he had to save his strength for what was to come—but then he saw images of Erin on the altar.

"Your daughter, Algeniz, killed my only love." Bon Deux's voice softened.

"Good!" Rogan chuckled. "If you then slew my baby girl, I suspect she died well, taking that cunt Maman Ezili with her. I will piss in Maman's eye sockets when I cross over the plain into the next world."

"Your daughter lives," Papa Bon Deux conceded. "I would kill myself to see her die."

"Go on then. Don't let me stop you."

Papa Bon Deux shook his head. "We shall face the fate of my

mate. She was consumed by our pet. A fitting sacrifice to Damballah, no?"

"I wouldn't know. I wager a privy bucket is a fine sacrifice for your little bat god."

"Damballah doesn't care if you are just a filthy killer or a pure beauty. His children care not how pretty their meals, as long as there is blood and gristle. In time, all power will flow from this spot and the world will be mine, because of Maman Ezili's final sacrifice. What resides inside that cocoon will not remain there for long. It will need to be fed and primed when it emerges. And while your son, using the body of your other son, searches for your daughter, I will be here to attend to it."

Rogan inched closer. "Are you trying to bore me to death?"

"You are clueless as to what I have in store, aren't you?"

Rogan looked at the cocoon. It seemed to move, as if breathing. "I know what lies inside. I've heard tales of such beasts. As for your plans, I care not for the folly of wizards."

"If you have heard of the Helvectia, then you are more astute than I had assumed. As for my plan, there's no way to stop it now. You see, once it emerges from this larval stage, I will finish training it. I will become its master. Not Karza. Not anyone. Only me."

Rogan nodded at the cocoon. "So, you'll betray my son and rule the world with that thing as your enforcer?"

"You know the tales of the Helvectia! You know how strong it will be. The men of this world will be powerless to stop it."

Rogan shook his head. "To think how we dreaded you. To think of all the fear your name invoked. And in the end, you're just another madman, whose plan will never succeed."

"You'll never know," Papa Bon Deux replied. "Because you'll be dead."

DRENCHED AND SHIVERING, JAVAN AND JASPER-THAL CREPT

into the courtyard of the temple of Rhiannon. They had heard a battle taking place only moments before, as they approached from a side alley, but the rain had prevented them from seeing what was taking place. Now, they discovered the aftermath—seven of Karza's soldiers butchered on the wet cobblestones. Brains squished beneath their boots as they examined the scene. A discarded scrotum. A fallen flail. Blood.

"It seems Rogan was here," Javan said. "He must be inside the temple."

"Dear God ..." Jasper-Thal gaped at the carnage. "He did all this by himself?"

"This is nothing. I suspect we'll find more bodies inside. Come along, he has need of us no matter what."

"I wish I were home," Jasper-Thal whined.

"How did you get so far away from it?"

"I was told to go out among men and spread the word that the world will soon end. So, I ran away from my parents and did."

"Let's hope you're wrong," Javan replied.

Shouts echoed behind them, followed by the clank of armor. A platoon of soldiers trotted toward the courtyard.

"Inside," Javan urged. "Hurry!"

"COME, ROGAN," PAPA BON DEUX LAUGHED. "WE ARE BOTH old men, but you are clearly my superior in size and strength. You, the legend of legends, who kills all, even his only true love, stand there cowering before me, reluctant to advance."

Rogan shook his damp gray-white mane. "I am indeed a killer, Bon Deux. With my bloody hands, I have killed everything that can walk or crawl on this rotten world. Men, women, and children —and yes, even the only woman I ever loved, Keevah, died by my hands. And now I am going to kill you."

"With vain boasts? You are not bound or in chains, and yet you stand there, trembling, no better than a tied dog."

"I'm not trembling in fear," Rogan said. "I tremble with anticipation."

The wizard's smile vanished.

Rogan raised his sword over his head with both hands and bellowed the name of his god.

"Woooodannnnn!"

Papa Bon Deux stepped backward, avoiding the lines on the floor, and began to mumble a quick recitation. His hands worked and twisted, making symbols in the air. He turned to run, but then paused. His eyes widened as he realized Rogan had tricked him. Instead of charging, Rogan flung the broadsword. It soared across the temple, spinning end over end, and then slammed into the wizard's chest, stopping him in mid-spell. The force of the blow knocked the sorcerer backward. He fell within an inch of the star on the floor. Still trying to finish the incantation, blood bubbled from his lips.

Rogan ran toward him, grabbed the wizard's fluttering hands, and squeezed. Papa Bon Deux's finger bones snapped like twigs. The sorcerer screamed, and more blood welled from his lips.

"Ssshhh," Rogan said, almost gently. "Be happy, wizard. I am sending you to see your bat god. Give Damballah my regards."

Standing, Rogan stared down at the writhing old man. He pulled his sword from Papa Bon Deux's chest, wiped the blade on the wizard's robes, and then stomped on his head with the heel of his boot until the sorcerer's skull split open like a melon.

The door crashed open. Rogan whirled, sword ready, and was surprised to see Javan and a younger boy, perhaps a few years older than Algeniz. The stranger seemed familiar. After a second, Rogan realized it was the crazy lad he'd been imprisoned with in the palace dungeon.

"Sire." Javan bowed.

Rogan nodded. "Took you long enough."

"My God," Jasper-Thal gasped, staring in astonishment at the gore-strewn floor.

"Your god takes no note of this," Rogan said. "We are on our own here."

"Not for long, sire." Javan slammed the door shut and bolted it. "A large group of soldiers are surrounding the temple."

"Close the doors, and bar them tight," Rogan instructed.

"God will protect us," Jasper-Thal said.

Rogan laughed. "Gods? Speak to me not of gods, little boy! They shall do as they always do ... sit on the sidelines and play with themselves. I don't need their protection."

Javan stepped forward and shook his uncle's hand. "It is good to see you again, sire."

"Aye," Rogan agreed. "I had wondered if you got free of those flying things."

"I seem to have as much trouble dying as you, uncle."

Before Rogan could respond, they heard a rustling sound coming from the temple attic. Dust swirled down upon their heads. Rogan's eyes narrowed as he studied the ceiling. Javan notched an arrow and waited to draw. Jasper-Thal nervously shifted his dagger from hand to hand.

"I wish to join the reunion," a small voice called.

"Algeniz!" Rogan's voice was thick with relief. "Are you safe, girl?"

"Yes, father. I'll climb down."

She descended from the attic and crossed the temple floor, warily avoiding the lines of the star. She glanced at the cocoon, and then paused to linger in front of Papa Bon Deux's corpse. After a moment, she spat on his face. Then she ran to her father. Rogan hugged her tight. When he looked up, he noticed Jasper-Thal staring at Algeniz as if he'd been struck by thunder. Despite everything, Rogan couldn't help but grin.

"What now, sire?" Javan asked.

Rogan broke off his embrace with his daughter and hefted his sword. "Now, with a little luck, we figure out how to destroy that thing in the middle of the star, and then kill this bastard son of mine once and for all."

Suddenly, the doors shook as Karza's soldiers began to batter them. The noise echoed throughout the temple. Then, there was a second sound. The four of them turned and saw the cocoon begin to split open.

"Repent," Jasper-Thal moaned. "I think our luck may be running out."

CHAPTER 14

ASSAULT ON ALBION

Thyssen had always been a great forager. A horse thief in his youth, he'd learned how to scrounge and make do with what he had—or what he could take. As they approached the capitol city, Thyssen took horses from the farms and various equestrian ranches in the outer lying areas of Albion, creating a makeshift auxiliary cavalry force that would certainly have numbers and mounts if not the best training as such.

The old general had been in the military since he was forcibly conscripted to serve a king almost fifty years before. Thyssen knew war and he understood tactics, not just learned from the table behind the lines, but what worked up close and on the field. He also understood the geography of Albion better than the usurper and his foreign legion. He knew the history of the land—the lows, the marshes, the soft spots, the sink holes, the fishing holes and the places to fuck in without being discovered. The instructions he gave his men as they marched in the rain, tutoring them for a time on guerilla tactics, was not his usual fare. Invading his own country, using his knowledge against it ... his anger burned hot.

He let the crazed berserker force from Thule attack first. Still smarting over the death of the princess betrothed to Rohain, the leader of the Thule forces charged his men toward the capital and was met by the largest forces of defense. The Cramonds followed behind them. Thyssen knew that Albion's military would condense more as the first insertion took place, folding in on the force of Thulites and the Cramond. Thyssen needed fodder and the berserkers provided the meat for the grinder. The invasion insertion via the north-western corner of Albion was the first stab into the land.

At Thyssen's command, Andraste rallied her forces for the third wave, barking instructions along rat lines of savages. Thyssen smiled at the filthy pagans, knowing that Karza had attained something he never could—getting the vast majority of Pryten warriors out of the wilderness at once. Oh, it would be a slaughter and Thyssen found himself on the other side, but it was a dream no one in the Albion military had ever hoped to accomplish. Seeing the forest empty across the land would be a great thing, the old general mused, but he had other things on his mind.

Thunder and lightning blasted across the sky, stretching from one horizon to the other. The rain fell in sheets, blown by harsh winds.

The Prytens attacked on either side of the Thulite and Cramond insertion. They possessed no lines or method, just a primal lust for blood and death. As he watched the battle rage from afar, and heard the howls and cries echoing across the countryside, Thyssen mourned the innocents slain and destroyed at the edges of the capitol by these hordes. As the fight progressed, an organized opposing force pressed the Prytens backward. At that moment, Andraste's Troglodytes appeared, as if from nowhere, seeming to materialize out of the bushes and trees. Thyssen still felt uneasy about using these beasts in battle, but he couldn't help but be impressed as they swept through the Albion resistance, cutting them down. He only hoped Andraste could reign the creatures in again lest they slaughter the civilians in their rampage.

Sitting next to him on a horse, Xuxan muttered in the language of Olmek-Tikal. Thyssen turned to the captain and suppressed a laugh. The foreigner was clearly unaccustomed to being on horse-back. To make matters worse, Zenata clung behind him in the saddle, clearly displeased with being sidelined at the rear of the procession while others went to battle.

"What did you say?" Thyssen asked.

"I said we use monsters to fight monsters," Xuxan replied. "It makes me uncomfortable."

"Aye," Thyssen agreed. "It does me, as well. But we don't need them any longer. It is time to send our ground forces in and flank Karza's troops with our cavalry. The bridge to the capital is our goal. If we can't take that, then we're fucked."

Xuxan didn't respond. Instead, the sea captain stared down at the battlefield. Thyssen followed his gaze, and noticed something disturbing—the Troglodytes had stopped their attack and seemed to be tearing at themselves, as if bewitched.

"What now?" Thyssen grumbled. "Magic?"

He gave the order for the ground troops and cavalry to advance. Then he observed that the downpour was slowly turning into a drizzle.

"This damned storm is letting up."

Zenata nodded. "Maybe luck is on our side."

The landscape rang with the sounds of dying.

BOONE REINED UP HIS MOUNT AS HIS CAVALRY WAS SET TO advance across an open meadow, hemmed in by an ancient tree line. Water dripped from the leaves and branches. Behind his group trailed a large cluster of Prytens on foot with Andraste in the lead.

"What is it?" she yelled. "Why have we stopped?"

Pointing the tip of his spear at the Troglodytes, Boone asked, "What ails them?"

Andraste rode forward toward the nearest creature. It looked at her, arms outstretched, as if pleading. Before she could reach it, the Troglodyte fell over and splintered onto the ground. All across the field, the other tree-beasts were doing the same. With a cry, Andraste leapt from her mount and knelt beside the nearest Troglodyte.

"They are full of termites," she shouted. "These bugs eat through their scales and flesh like a small army."

"The trees," Boone said. "They must be lousy with them!"

Andraste and the Prytens exchanged worried looks before she said to Boone, "I've never seen such a plague, nor have I seen them move so fast. What accounts for it?"

"I've heard of such things," Boone replied. "In Karza's homeland. Perhaps they imported them here for just such a situation— or to use when he eventually invaded your land."

"Curse them," Andraste raged. "I'll feed him his own balls!"

Boone nodded, losing all hope that the Troglodytes would be of any further help. His expression became somber as he watched Andraste weep over their fragmented corpses.

"Advance," he ordered, glancing back at their forces. "We can weep later ... if we're still alive."

Both the day and the battle progressed. Thyssen's chest tightened as he saw the inevitable scenario start to play out. Though he directed some of his troops toward more obscure crossing points of the river shielding the capitol city, fighting and fleeing Albion regulars caused most of his forces to pursue them— allowing Karza's men to mount a defense of the main bridge.

"Damn their eyes and asses!" Thyssen fumed. A siege wasn't what he wanted. He had not the manpower or the supplies for such an endeavor.

"We can surround them," Xuxan suggested. "Take out all outlining forces! We can forage from the smaller villages and farmsteads. In time, we will wear them down."

Thyssen snorted. "True enough. In time, a siege would wear

them down. But Rogan, Javan, and Algeniz are in there, and I reckon time is not on their side."

Sighing, Thyssen gave the order for all forces to converge on the bridge, informing his commanders to let the Thulite and Pryten hordes swarm the causeway first.

"Either we swamp it and force entry into the city," he told Xuxan, "or this is where we fail."

Zenata frowned in apparent confusion. "You claim to hate Andraste's savages and love that fair city. You would let them into it first?"

Thyssen pointed as the Prytens charged the bridge, Queen Andraste riding victorious and tall before them, while Boone, the cavalry, and the ground troops held back.

"Yes, girl," he answered Zenata. "That's exactly what I'm doing. The city isn't so fair now. And neither am I."

Xuxan shook his head. "They will be crushed between Karza's army and our troops when you advance ... won't they?"

Thyssen winked at him. "Every damned one of them."

Xuxan's eyes widened. Then he smiled and shook his head in admiration.

Thyssen turned to Zenata. "My son is fond of you. And I can't take you moping about. You wanted revenge on that Pryten bitch? I just got it for you. Say thank you. I only hope Javan is alive to appreciate the gesture, too."

Laughing, Zenata clapped her hands. Then she turned toward the city, and hoped for the same thing.

CHAPTER 15

ANOTHER BASTARD SON

"Give me a hand, damn you, boys," Rogan barked at Javan and Jasper-Thal. He stood staring at the cocoon, as the Helvectia beast thrust one arm from the webbing and flexed.

Jasper-Thal shook his head. "What exactly do you want us to do?"

"Ask Javan," Rogan said. "He's more knowledgeable about these things than me. And why do you sound more in control of your wits than when we were imprisoned together?"

"I got better. But need I remind you that even if we survive this day, the one true God will soon flood this Earth?"

Rogan scowled. "Now you sound more like yourself."

Another long arm ripped free of the webbing. A chittering noise emerged from the cocoon, almost drowning out the sounds of pounding at the door. The bar rattled in its hasps as an axe blade bit through the wood.

"The soldiers have almost broken through," Algeniz warned.

"Sire," Javan said, "I do not know if this demon can be caged by the star any longer."

"Then let's kill the bitch before it gets free."

Brandishing his sword, Rogan crossed over the blood lines and stalked into the center of the sigil. Javan, Algeniz, and Jasper-Thal glanced at each other. Then, Javan followed his uncle into the star. Cringing, Algeniz did the same.

"Stay behind your cousin, girl," Rogan cautioned.

"I shall protect you, Princess," Jasper-Thal whispered.

"I do not require your protection," she snapped.

The cocoon split along its length, and the Helvectia tumbled out, weak and mewling. Its wings were plastered to its back, still wet and dripping with mucous. It tried to stand on wobbly, spider-like legs, but then fell back to the floor. It raised an elongated head and gazed at Rogan and his kin with yellow, red-rimmed eyes. Then it reached for them, tentatively, almost gently.

"It is different now," Algeniz observed, her voice hushed with wonder. "It not only looks different—it behaves differently, as well."

"It ..." Javan gaped. "It's like an infant."

"I've killed babies before," Rogan said, raising his sword. "They die easy."

Before he could deliver the blow, the doors crashed open in an explosion of splinters and shards of wood. A dozen bellowing soldiers rushed into the temple, charging forward with weapons drawn. They stumbled and fell silent when they saw the Helvectia, but were relentlessly pushed forward as more of their comrades tried to enter.

Squawking with fright, Jasper-Thal retreated into the confines of the star. He glanced back and forth between the demon and the enemy troops. The blood drained from his face.

"This thing is an affront to God!"

"Makes me wonder why He created it, then." Rogan tossed his sword from hand to hand, eyeing the onrushing troops.

With a noise like an enraged elephant, the Helvectia tottered to its feet, towering over all in the room. It seemed to have forgotten about the three men standing closest to it, and focused instead on the soldiers. With more forces pushing through the doorway, the warriors in the front of the charge had no choice but to step over the lines of the star. Roaring, the Helvectia spread its wings, nearly knocking Rogan to the floor. Claws extended, it stomped toward the soldiers.

"Quickly," Rogan whispered, motioning to Javan, Algeniz, and Jasper-Thal. "This way."

The four of them ran to the other side of the sigil and stepped outside of its confines. While the Helvectia tore through the cluster of troops spilling into the star, Rogan and Javan flanked the edges of the room, cutting down any soldier who came their way. Jasper-Thal stood at the rear of the temple, watching in horror as both man and demon butchered and hacked. Algeniz positioned herself in front of him, as if to protect the heretic. Steel rang. Arrows flew. Talons shredded and tore. Men died, shrieking as their blood sprayed. When it was over, the floor ran red, obscuring the lines of the star.

"Now for this thing," Rogan rasped. Turning his attention back to the Helvectia.

The beast turned at the sound of his voice, and cocked its head. It made a trilling noise in the back of its throat, and then began to lick the blood from its claws.

"It's afraid to attack me," Rogan boasted.

"No, sire." Javan's tone was one of astonishment. "I think it ... it sees you as its master, perhaps?"

"Me? I didn't summon this fucking thing. This is all Papa Bon Deux's work."

"I am not a wizard," Javan replied, "and I don't pretend to understand the ways of Damballah's magic, but based on what I remember from university, and on Papa Bon Deux and Maman Ezili's boastings, and judging by its own indifference to us, I would say this creature obeys you. Maybe because you were the first thing it saw when it emerged from the cocoon? Maybe it thinks you gave it these soldiers as sacrifice? Maybe it views you as its father."

"Another bastard son?"

"Or maybe ..." Javan trailed off.

"Or maybe what? Spit it out, lad."

"Or maybe there is something of Akibeel still left inside, sire."

Rogan was quiet for a moment, surveying the Helvectia. Then he cleared his throat. The creature turned its attention back to him again. Rogan shivered.

"Do you understand me?"

Slowly, the Helvectia nodded.

"And you serve me?"

The beast made a sound like a cross between purring and cooing.

"You see these men on the floor? The ones we just killed?"

The creature glanced down at the mutilated corpses and then back up at Rogan. The old barbarian gestured with his sword at the smashed doorway.

"You go out there and kill anyone you see that looks like them. Understand me? Kill them all. Then, and only then, you may go freely into the world and find your fate."

Grunting, the creature raised its head and roared, seeming to shake the temple's rafters. Then, in two long bounds, it crossed over the now blood-covered lines of the star and lunged toward the door. Pausing only to squeeze its bulk through the opening, it stepped into the courtyard, spread its wings, and took flight.

"What have you done?" Jasper-Thal gasped. "You have unleashed an abomination upon the world. What happens when it is finished with Rohain's soldiers?"

"His name is not Rohain," Algeniz said. "He is Karza, perverting the flesh of my brother."

Ignoring her, Jasper-Thal kept his attention on Rogan. "Do you know how many innocents will die because of what you've done?"

Rogan shrugged. "If the gods don't want their followers killed, then they should have stopped me."

"There is but one God," Jasper-Thal argued.

"I could name hundreds if my mind were clear, but who cares? You are young and will not mind me any more than Algeniz does."

"You've seen the works of the devil in this Damballah. Why is it you refuse to believe in a God?"

"Never said I didn't believe in one. If your God is upset with me, then let Him come to me, just like all the others. I'll kill Him, too."

Jasper-Thal stood speechless as Rogan crept toward the door. Javan and Algeniz followed after him. Shoulders slumped in resignation, slunk along behind them. They walked out into the courtyard, emerging into the sounds of a city under attack. Javan scurried up a fruit tree and looked out over the streets and alleyways.

"What do you see?" Rogan called.

"Soldiers fleeing. Some holding positions. Regular folk running around in panic, like ants."

"Wodan be praised," Algeniz sighed.

Rogan tousled her hair and smiled. "More like Thyssen, Boone and Andraste be praised."

"It's madness," Jasper-Thal proclaimed.

"It's life," Rogan countered. "It's war. Death. The natural ending for all things is death. Who knows? Maybe we will see what mine looks like before the sun sets. Be ready, yours may be waiting for you today, as well."

Javan climbed back down. "Karza will realize his wizard is dead soon."

"Aye." Rogan stared out across the city, toward the palace. "Upon everyone's life, a little pain must fall. Heh. My father used to say that. Do you hear it, Javan? Do you hear it, Algeniz? Do you hear the call from your blood? Can you hear a thousand warriors in your veins, marching, demanding a fight? Can you hear the call to battle?"

Both of them nodded.

"These traitors corrupted everything I hold dear." Rogan's eyes narrowed. "They've defiled my blood and the ones I love. But there is still one left to deal with."

Javan readied his bow. "You will not face him alone, sire."

"I must." Rogan paused. "But you three can come along, if you like. I could use a cheering section."

They started across the courtyard and down a winding path through the garden, that led to a gate in the walls. Rogan glanced back at the former temple of Rhiannon.

"Wish we could burn it to the ground," he muttered.

"What would that solve?" Jasper asked.

Rogan shrugged. "It would make me feel better. It would bring me joy."

He then opened the gate and stepped out onto the city streets, jogging toward the palace. The three youths followed him at a distance.

CHAPTER 16
HAIL TO THE KING

The once-fair city of Albion now resembled a charnel house. The streets were awash in blood and littered with corpses and severed limbs. Homes and businesses burned, and smoke rose high into the air, blotting out the sun and turning the afternoon hazy and gray. Rogan, Javan, Algeniz, and Jasper-Thal saw evidence of Thyssen's troops—soldiers who had been stabbed, slashed, impaled, pierced with arrows or simply bludgeoned to death. But they were also very aware that they walked in the wake of the Helvectia beast, judging by the number of pulped and mangled soldiers they came across.

They walked for a long time, until they came to the main street of Albion's capital. It was there, surrounded by blood splatters, bodies and the ruins of destroyed shops, that they encountered Karza and his remaining guards. The pretend King and his men had just finished off a platoon of Thyssen's ground troops, and seemed to be catching their breath.

"We still have to find my father and sister," Karza ordered. "Let us return to the temple of Rhiannon with haste."

"But, my lord," complained one of the soldiers, "surely they are gone by now, or killed by that monstrosity therein?"

Shrugging, Karza spun around and slit the man's throat. Blood sprayed across his face and armor. Grinning, he licked his lips and faced the rest of his troops.

"Are there any others among you who do not wish to continue the search?"

"They won't have to look far," Rogan shouted.

Karza turned, eyes widening when he saw Rogan, Javan, Algeniz, and Jasper-Thal standing side-by-side in the street.

"You and me," Rogan said. "These other men stand back, or Javan will cut them down before they can move."

"Oh, if any of them try to interfere, I'll kill them myself. But you seem to be at a disadvantage, father. You're practically naked."

Chuckling, Karza removed his chain mail shirt and cast off the light armor on his forearms.

"Rohain would have never been stupid enough to remove his armor," Rogan said.

"I am not Rohain."

"No," Rogan agreed, his voice resigned. "You are not. I watched Rohain breathe his first breath with that body. I'll watch you breathe your last with it, as well."

"Shall we begin?"

Rogan shrugged. "I'm not getting any younger."

The men behind Karza stepped back, clearing space in the street. Javan, Algeniz, and Jasper-Thal did the same. Javan kept an arrow notched, waiting for any sign of deceit, but Karza's troops seemed mindful of their master's warning. Karza gripped his broadsword, letting it drift over his vision a few times as he looked at his father.

Rogan stood alone, sword in hand, boots squared to his shoulders. The old warrior and his fearsome persona had frightened masses and caused many men to rush to their deaths in his time. Rogan felt well aware Karza knew all the tales and had studied him. Still, Rogan took the first move. Usually, the fight came to him, but now he stepped forward, looked Karza in Rohain's eyes, and slashed to the right. Anticipating the block move from Karza's sword, Rogan let the blow be defended and swung around, only to be blocked on the left.

Karza stabbed low, aiming for Rogan's calf. Rogan swept his sword down and away, causing his opponent to spread his arms. The old warrior kicked at Karza's exposed midsection, but the younger man skipped backwards, avoiding him.

With one hand, Rogan made a forward thrust with his broadsword, aiming for Karza's heart. Karza easily slapped the blow down. His eyes flared when he saw that Rogan's sword nearly slipped out of his grip. In that second, he redoubled his effort and moved forward, giving the sword an extra slap down. Too late, Karza realized his error, for his own weapon crossed Rogan's and touched the ground. Rogan gripped his own weapon fast and stomped on the section of Karza's sword crossing his. The angle and leverage were perfect and the sword popped from the mad King's grip. Karza tried to retreat, but Rogan's left hand darted out, delivering a devastating upper cut. Karza's nose popped, but no blood came out.

Cursing that his father disarmed him with such ease, Karza drew a short sword from his side scabbard. He eyed Rogan, who stood over the fallen broadsword.

"Whenever you are ready," Rogan said, his tone dripping with mock patience.

Karza charged. Slashing on both sides, Rogan was forced to use the heavy sword to block each blow. Karza's momentum kept pressing Rogan backward, testing his stamina. Karza continued the assault, refusing to slow. When he deflected the broadsword away from Rogan's body, he elbowed his father in the ribs. Rogan coughed, feeling the pain stab through his upper chest. Trying to bring his sword down on his son, Rogan didn't see the incoming fist until it crashed into his jaw. Ears ringing, he stumbled backward and tried to clear his vision.

Repeatedly, Karza tried the assault to each side of Rogan. Again, the old warrior refused to weaken and give up his great sword. However, it was clear to all observers that dueling with such a big blade was taxing the aged warrior. Suddenly, Rogan took a knee and Karza slashed his weapon down, pinning his father's broadsword to his chest. He pressed his forearm over Rogan's face, but yelped as the elder fighter's teeth sank into his wrist. He jumped back, releasing his sword, but took Rogan's broadsword with it. Unarmed, the two men faced each other anew.

Rogan didn't hesitate, stepping forward and trying to hit his son with a backhand swipe. He missed, due to Karza's agility, but the blow was meant to offset the real mode of attack ... Rogan's boot to Karza's groin. Karza's knees slapped together, stopping the blow from landing. The younger man laughed.

"You look tired, old man."

When Rogan didn't respond, Karza laughed louder.

Arms flailing, the two men grappled. Rogan yanked his leg back to support himself. Karza went for the throat, both hands on the corded muscle. Quickly, Rogan grabbed Karza's face in his hands and wrenched to each side, as if he were tearing apart a sheet of paper. The move worked. Shrieking, Karza released his throat.

The younger man gripped his father in a fast embrace, pinning his massive arms down. Then, elevating him slightly, Karza threw Rogan to the ground. Though stunned, Rogan rolled with the move. Karza interlocked his fingers and used them as a bludgeon, dropping his full weight behind the shot to Rogan's skull. Head shaking, Rogan took the blow in full and followed with an uppercut jab to Karza's throat. Gagging, the mad king stumbled back, breaking off his attack.

Now it was Rogan's turn to laugh again, as blood dribbled off his chin. "You'll have to do better than that."

As Rogan rose up, Karza hunched over and threw himself forward, spearing Rogan's midsection. Both men tumbled back on the ground, but Rogan used his legs to throw off Karza. Rolling up to all fours, Rogan had no time to get his bearings as his son was on him again, holding him in a front face lock, twisting his head. Rogan's eyes widened. He recognized the move. Karza's legs braced as he prepared to throw his weight and break Rogan's neck.

Abruptly, Rogan used his weight and went flat. Slipping from Karza's grip, he rolled onto his back and sprang to his feet, landing a hard blow to his son's jaw. Karza paused, stunned by the blow. Rogan grabbed his legs and pulled. Unbalanced, Karza fell to the street, shoulder slamming down hard. Scrambling like a spider, Rogan climbed on top of him and struck him again in the face. Legs writhing, Karza's body shifted. He threw Rogan off, effectively reversing the move and ending up on top of his father.

"Come on, sire," Javan yelled. "Take him!"

"Kill him," Algeniz urged. "Remember what they did to Teran and Erin! What they did to us all."

"Oh, God," Jasper-Thal prayed, hands clasped fervently, "give this pagan warrior your strength and blessing."

Karza's soldiers responded with yells and jeers of their own.

Paying no mind, Karza slammed his shin into Rogan's groin and straddled his body. He swung at Rogan, but Rogan blocked the move with his arm, pushing Karza backwards. Rogan hooked his legs around his son's head and pulled him up off him. Once Karza was up high enough, Rogan smacked him square in the crotch and threw him to the left. Clutching his groin, Karza staggered, trying to stay up on his knees.

Rogan turned, looking for a weapon. When he went for Karza's discarded short sword, his son scrambled after Rogan's broadsword. Karza gained the weapon first. One of his soldiers threw a shield to him. Karza snatched it up with his free hand. As he did so, Javan put an arrow through the soldier's eye. Still staggered by the shot to his groin, Karza's steps were unsteady and awkward. Rogan speared him in the knees with the tip of the short sword, sending Karza to the ground with no weapon again. Javan covered the rest of the guards, but none of them moved to assist their king.

Trying to get his breath, Rogan put his hand to his waist and staggered backward. He had thought the injuries to Rohain's knees would slow Karza down, but the younger man charged again, moving silently. Karza swung the sword, but when Rogan parried,

Karza shoved the edge of the shield under the older man's left armpit and pushed upward. A loud pop echoed as Rogan's shoulder came out of joint, dislocating.

Throwing his head back, Rogan screamed. Karza stepped toward him, sword raised, and aimed for Rogan's heart, but Rogan swiveled at the last moment and drove his own weapon into his son's abdomen. Karza gasped. Eye to eye, father and son exchanged expressions of agony. Slowly, Karza let the shield and sword slip from his hands. Rogan shoved him free of the sword, which slipped out of Karza's body with a wet squelch.

Rogan turned to Jasper-Thal. "Boy, take my daughter around the corner. I do not want her to see this."

Algeniz protested, struggling to remain, but Jasper-Thal was able to lead her around the bend of a street.

Karza staggered, blood flowing through his fingers as he covered the wound. He looked from side to side, desperate for a weapon. He motioned at his soldiers.

"You men ... attack him!"

The enemy troops glanced from their king to Rogan and then back to Karza again. As one, they turned and fled.

Rogan advanced. Left arm dangling useless as his side, Rogan turned his back to his son and reached behind the younger man's head with his right arm. The swift move, to reverse headlock him and suddenly drop to his backside, had the desired effect. Javan gasped as Karza's neck snapped. Rogan released him, letting Karza's limp form fall to the street. Javan crept closer, and saw that Karza still breathed, despite his broken neck.

Picking up the broadsword, Rogan held it level to his waist. He didn't need both hands for the coming task, and yet he hesitated. Javan watched him, standing there and staring down at the body on the ground, at the bastard son inhabiting the body of another, beloved son, at the king inside the other king.

Minutes passed and still Rogan did not move. Javan took a step closer, clearing his throat. When Rogan looked up, Javan was shocked to see tears in his eyes.

"Javan ... I ..."

Making a slight bow, Javan reached out and took the broadsword from Rogan's grip. Never before had Rogan, son of Jarek, been so easily disarmed. The old man didn't move as Javan raised the sword and let it fall. Though the weapon was heavy, and Javan strong, the blow wasn't delivered by a seasoned warrior. The sword only sank through Rohain's muscled neck and stuck to the bones. His body jerked as Javan drew the sword out and swung a second time, finishing the act. This time, Rohain's head lolled off and rolled to one side. Jets of blood splashed the long dreadlock tresses as his heart beat its last.

Standing in stony silence, Rogan swallowed hard, but his tears had dried.

Javan picked up Rohain's head by the scalp. He glanced over his shoulder, hearing the approach of a large body of people.

Javan inserted the blade through the bottom of Rohain's neck. He then held up the sword and offered it to Rogan.

"A crowd is coming, sire. I'd hate to be lynched for this."

Rogan took the sword and held the head up in the dwindling sunlight. He understood Javan's words, for it was important, win or lose, for the masses to think Rogan had killed the king.

"I am your obedient servant, sire. No thanks are necessary."

"None will be forthcoming," Rogan muttered.

As Jasper-Thal led Algeniz back out from behind the shops nearby, a large group of the citizenry of Albion's capital appeared, intermingled with Thyssen's forces. Rogan noticed that there were no Prytens, however.

Many who were not there would later claim to have been in attendance to witness the Kelt savage Rogan raise the head of his son on a sword and call out to his pagan god Wodan. Many would tell how Princess Algeniz was the first to kneel at her father's boots and weep. But all testified in truth that they agreed and conceded as Javan faced the crowd and proclaimed:

"All hail the king, Rogan the Great."

The masses knelt and bowed to the warrior before them,

holding up the head of his own son on a sword ... and clutching a bloody crown in his hand.

RUBBING HIS LEFT SHOULDER, ROGAN SAID, "YOU ALWAYS WERE a piss-poor field surgeon."

"Next time," Thyssen replied, "I'll leave yer sorry ass with a dislocated shoulder.

As Rogan tried to stretch his shoulder, he looked at those assembled at the palace gate.

Boone and Andraste arrived from a different route than Thyssen, who was allowed across the main bridge once word swept the city that Rohain and the wizards were dead. Andraste rushed to Rogan and fell at his feet, more in an exhausted stagger than any sort of reverence.

"He killed them all!" She turned and cursed Thyssen. "He slew my people, all the Prytens!"

Rogan glanced at Thyssen. "Did he now?"

Thyssen shrugged. "Got as many as we could."

"He ... father ..." she stammered.

Rogan sighed. "Father, is it now? You were all ashes, guile and snatch power before. I hated your filthy people, their gods and their ways."

As two soldiers pulled her away, she screamed, "You did this! I name you, Rogan the slayer, butcher, using him as your weapon of extermination."

Ignoring her, Rogan turned to Thyssen. "What is the standing order for all Prytens in the city limits?"

Thyssen said sternly, "Execution."

"Then see to it."

Thyssen nodded at the soldiers holding Andraste. "You heard the king."

"Hold," Rogan called. "You men ... find Zenata, the foreign woman with one breast. Allow her to carry it out."

Algeniz pushed forward through the crowd, gasping. "Father! You can't have her killed. She's your daughter."

Rogan shook his head. "No, she isn't."

Indignant, the little girl balled up her fists. "Why do you say that now?"

"Because, she is no more my daughter than Karza and Karac were my sons." He knelt, and cupped Algeniz's face in his hands. "You won't understand now, but you will when you get older. You are my daughter. Javan is my nephew. That is enough for me."

Thyssen pulled Rogan aside. "You aren't staying here, are you?"

"No. I really cannot stay here."

"Better a realm in tatters than one under the heel of those bastards. Andraste got her wish. Albion is in ruins, sort of. You could turn things around again."

"Why stay?" Rogan asked. "I'm turning the crown over to you, Thyssen. Look what that crown has done to my kin. It makes peace a thin blanket indeed. You have seen how my past infected Karza and Karac and Andraste, and what it wrought for Teran and Erin. I would not see Algeniz suffer the same fate."

"Doesn't seem to have infected Javan, after all the traveling he's done with you."

"That's because Javan has much of his mother in him."

"Aye." Thyssen nodded proudly. "That he does."

Rogan glanced back to Algeniz, and saw Jasper-Thal consoling her. He smiled, watching the two embrace. Slowly, Rogan walked over to them.

"You favor my daughter, young Jasper-Thal?"

"Um ..." Jasper stammered. "Yes, sir."

"Then take care of her, boy, forever. See that she has sons and that they never forget where they came from."

Jasper nodded. "I will save her from even the end of the Earth."

"See that you do, by Wodan, or my shade will haunt you forever."

Rogan then knelt and put his right arm around Algeniz. "Be

strong, little one. You make me proud with your strength. Someday you will understand."

Wiping a tear away, Algeniz smiled. "Perhaps I already do. My father is as he is."

Rogan nodded.

Algeniz took the long cord from her neck and offered it to him. "Mother cast this rune in my name when she carried me."

"I know." Taking the necklace, Rogan placed it over his head and pulled his long hair out. "You shall be with me always."

"I love you, Papa."

Rogan embraced her awkwardly, favoring his shoulder.

"Where will you go and what will you do?" Jasper-Thal asked.

"Me? I go to face the greatest adventure of my life ..."

Rogan turned his back on Albion forever.

CHAPTER 17
THE LAST GREAT ADVENTURE

Once again, with Xuxan from Olmek-Tikal guiding the vessel, and his crew at their stations, Rogan cast his line into the shifting waters of the vast, deep sea.

"Now, Javan," the old warrior said as he fixed his boots and set himself down. "If you can tear yourself away from Zenata for a moment, hand me that skin of wine and I'll teach you the true art of fishing."

EPILOGUE

ONE GOD'S PROMISE

The storyteller finished his yarn and leaned back on the ship to rest.

"Father ..." Magog looked out at the blue, almost translucent waves. "Father, are you saying that our mother, Algeniz, was almost sacrificed to Damballah?"

"Yes."

Gomer leaned forward. "Tell us more! Did Grandfather encounter more devils? I heard the story that he visited the Land of Nod!"

"That's a tale for another day, my boys. We must tend the animals."

"But, father," Magog persisted. "I still don't understand why the people of Albion called you Jasper-Thal when your name is Noah."

"As I have told you before, it is how they said my name when I took the tale of the end of the world to the corners of the Earth. No one listened when I told them to repent, and that's why only we are spared the cataclysm."

Japheth stared out at the water while the rest of his brothers clambered to their feet.

"Father," he asked. "Do you think Rogan could still be alive out there? Was he perhaps spared, as well?"

His father watched the waves rise and fall, but when he turned back to his son, he did not answer.

ACKNOWLEDGMENTS

Our thanks to Paul Goblirsch and Thunderstorm Books; Jason Sizemore, Lesley Conner, and Apex Book Company; Charles Rutledge; Mark Sylva, Tod Clark, Stephen McDornell, and Mike Acquavella.

Brian would like to thank Mary SanGiovanni, Cathy Gonzalez, Cassandra Burnham, Dave Thomas, Mike Lombardo, and Stephen Kozeniewski.

Steven would like to thank Laura Kitchell, Brady Allen, Bob Freeman, Minh, Chris and Angie Fulbright, Ron Kelly, John August Shrewsbury and Aaron K. Shrewsbury, and Peter Welmerink.

ABOUT THE AUTHORS

STEVEN L. SHREWSBURY lives, works, and writes in rural Illinois. Over three hundred and sixty of his short stories have been published in print or electronically, along with over one hundred poems. His novels include *Godforsaken, Overkill, Thrall, Bedlam Unleashed, Hawg, Tormentor, Stronger Than Death, Hell Billy, Bag Magick*, and many more—all running the gamut from sword and sorcery to historical fantasy to horror. A husband and father, he loves books, British television programs, guns, movies, politics, sports, and hanging out with his family. He looks for brightness wherever it may hide.

BRIAN KEENE writes novels, comic books, short fiction, and occasional journalism for money. He is the author of over fifty books, mostly in the horror, crime, and dark fantasy genres. His 2003 novel, *The Rising*, is often credited with inspiring pop culture's current interest in zombies. He has won numerous awards and honors, including the 2014 World Horror Grandmaster Award, 2001 Bram Stoker Award for Nonfiction, 2003 Bram Stoker Award for First Novel, 2004 Shocker Award for Book of the Year, and Honors from United States Army International Security Assistance Force in Afghanistan and Whiteman A.F.B. (home of the B-2 Stealth Bomber) 509th Logistics Fuels Flight. The father of two sons, Keene lives in rural Pennsylvania.